Endorsements

"Betty Busch takes the tool of serendipity to form a wonderful narrative of romantic comedy which keeps the reader intrigued even when they may guess what the next twist in plot is going to serve up for them. Very satisfying volume." – Millard Ray Howington, New Ellenton, South Carolina, Poet and Playwright.

"Rendezvous, is a hilarious read for anyone who needs an escape from the trials of real life! Busch has expertly woven into the story delightfully charming characters, which capture the true nature of family, love and friendships." – Janet Swope Wade, Aiken, South Carolina, Poet and Author.

"Rendezvous With a Perfect Stranger" was so much fun to read. It captured my attention in the first page or two, and so many times, I laughed out loud. The characters jumped off the page as I was reading." – Sharon Johnson, Retired English Teacher, South Aiken High School, Aiken, South Carolina.

Rendezvous with a Perfect Stranger

Betty Rollins Busch

WESTBOW·
PRESS
A DIVISION OF THOMAS NELSON
& ZONDERVAN

This is a work of fiction, and none of the people are real, except Katie, a
beautiful golden retriever is based on a friend's universal blood donor.

WestBow Press books may be ordered through booksellers or by contacting:

WestBow Press
A Division of Thomas Nelson & Zondervan
1663 Liberty Drive
Bloomington, IN 47403
www.westbowpress.com
1 (866) 928-1240

ISBN: 978-1-4908-1976-1 (sc)
ISBN: 978-1-4908-1977-8 (hc)
ISBN: 978-1-4908-1975-4 (e)

Library of Congress Control Number: 2013922446

Printed in the United States of America.

WestBow Press rev. date: 3/7/2014

4-12-14

Lynn:

Thank you so much for your support and your friendship

Enjoy the "Rendezvous."

Betty Rollins Busch

In Memory of Katie 1989-2001

Acknowledgements

My sincere gratitude goes to my children, Chris and Allison, who keep me humble by giving me the benefit of their forthright comments. I also give thanks to members of the Aiken Whiskey Road Chapter of South Carolina Writers Workshop for their support in my writing especially to Linda Kleckley Shaffer, Ph.D, Author, and Phyllis Maclay, Author, for their critiques and advice. My appreciation goes to Sharon Johnson, my friend and retired English teacher, who gave her expertise in correcting my spelling and grammar giving Rendezvous the final touch. I have dedicated this book to Katie, the beautiful golden retriever that in real life was a universal blood donor who was faithful in giving to other dogs when the need occurred, and appreciation to Shirley Jones Dyer, her owner, who allowed Katie to come into this story and save the life of fictitious, Fancy.

Chapter 1

Francine tapped the crystal of her watch, not that she doubted it worked, for it reflected the same time as the big clock on the wall of Joe's Bar and Grill. Her blind date was thirty-five minutes late. She mentally kicked herself for agreeing to the terms of her housemates' deal. They'd promised to leave her alone about getting back into the dating game if she would date three men, one each of their choosing.

Instead of following her own instincts, Francine agreed to their deal. For her third and final date, she'd had her long raven tresses done in a different style. The new black dress with spaghetti straps, gathers softly at her tiny waist, and the hemline just above her knees, swung gracefully. Her medium heels brought her height up to five-seven. She'd found the cologne from two of her housemates, Lillie and Marcie, a bit overwhelming. Francine opted for the light fragrance that Debbie offered, sprayed it into the air and allowed it to settle over her.

Here she was, sitting alone in a bar, waiting for some stranger who would probably be as unlikely a match for her as the first two blind dates. She was having second, third and fourth thoughts. With her finger, she swirled the melting ice in her ginger ale.

It was then a man hurried through the front door and headed straight toward her. He was about six feet tall and looked fabulous in a dark suit and gray tie. Black curly hair fell across his forehead.

No doubt, this was her date, Mark. She surprised herself as she straightened and thought, "*Not bad.*"

The man reached her side, with no apology, leaned in between Francine and the patron on the next stool, and said to the bartender, "A cool one, Joe."

"Well, it's about time you got here. You're thirty-five minutes late!" Francine slid from the stool as she almost shrieked. "And you're going to take the time for a beer?"

He seemed surprised and answered, "Excuse me?"

"Excuse you? I repeat. You're thirty-five minutes late. Let's get this over with." Francine headed toward the door. "Are you coming?"

She heard the man say to Joe, "Make that a soda."

He caught up with her just outside the door. "Where are we going?"

Both took advantage of the bit of daylight left to give each other a good once over. His eyes skimmed over her from top-to-toe and back, resting on her face.

Francine glared at him ignoring his baffled look. "What do you mean, where are we going? Didn't you make reservations? We'll never find a place to eat this late." Francine tried to focus on being angry, but facing him, she was pleased that her quick survey revealed he was pleasant to the eye. The man's shoulders filled the tailored suit – a perfect fit.

His slow, easy smile replaced the puzzled frown, causing soft wrinkles to form about the corners of his green eyes. "Hmm." She murmured as she made note of the *green eyes with black hair.* She guessed his age to be about thirty-five, the exact time of his tardiness.

There were a few moments of silence as she watched him running his hands through those black curls that plopped right back onto his forehead. She surmised that his olive skin was too smooth to be other than natural.

"I'm sorry. Are we going to dinner?" he asked.

She had no way of knowing that he'd spent the previous three hours debating with corporate executives over a merger. In addition, he was in dire need of a diversion, and his relieved glance around the parking lot reassured him that she was not part of a plot to mug him nor was she a lady of the evening.

"Dinner is the game plan. Didn't Debbie explain anything to you?"

"Not really." Squinting, he stared down at her, drawing his green eyes together beneath thick smooth eyebrows.

"Thank goodness you're the last one," she snapped at him.

"The last one?"

"The last blind date."

"The last blind date?"

"Where is your car?"

"My car?"

"Do you have to repeat everything I say? This date is supposed to be over at eleven o'clock sharp and it only includes dinner." The words dropped in the air like lead. "Let's get started if you don't mind." With arms crossed, she tapped her foot on the pavement as she looked around the parking lot. "Well, where's your car?"

"Right over there." He pointed to a silver Jaguar.

"A Jaguar? You rented a Jag?"

"Why no. It's my car."

"That's something, anyway."

She felt him watching her as she hurried to the passenger's side and without waiting for his assistance, opened the door, and slid onto the seat.

Spurred into action, he crushed the cup and pushed it into a litterbag before leaning over to help with her seat belt.

"Where do you think we'll eat? Remember I plan on paying my share." She ran the words together as the soft fragrance he wore, which was "clean and fresh, teased her senses." A man who used more cologne than Francine did, always turned her off. The thought crossed her mind that his aftershave was not in the same category with the cheap stuff Jerry wore.

"I know a place you and Debbie would approve of." He smiled before closing his door.

She relaxed somewhat during the short ride to the most exclusive restaurant in town. "I can't afford to eat here." Francine gasped. "I couldn't even afford half of whatever it would cost. Besides, we'll never get a table without reservations. Keep driving. Get fast food for all I care. Let's get this over with."

"Let's give this place a try. My treat."

"I refuse to be obligated." She was tempted to use one of her mother's favorite words, "*beholden*."

"Not to worry. This is a treat for me as well."

Before Francine could respond, two young men, one to help her from the car and the other to park it, were opening the doors.

"Hi, Jack!" the boy on the driver's side said.

Jack must be a nickname. She allowed him to take her elbow and guide her inside.

"Hello, Jack." The host led them to a table near the front of the dance floor where several couples were moving in slow fashion to the music of a full orchestra.

"Why is everyone calling you Jack? That can't be a nickname for Mark."

"Universal nickname," he said. She couldn't read his thoughts. "So Mark must be the jerk who stood this beauty up." He brushed his shoulder as if to rid himself of the tiny devil that might be sitting there. He'd worry about the consequences of not acknowledging her mistake later.

Once they'd given their drink orders, Francine was at a loss for further conversation and feeling a bit ashamed of her harshness. After all, he had brought her to *Ye Olde Dutch Inn*, the finest restaurant in town; He drove a Jag, and smelled wonderful. These were real plusses, pushing Debbie's choice over the top.

"What?" she asked in response to his bemused stare.

"Just wondering if you would tell me all about this date."

"Didn't Debbie explain anything?"

"No."

"What part did she explain so I'll know where to start."

"It would be best if you start from the beginning, so I'll have a clear picture. I want to be sure of what's expected."

Francine settled back in the chair, refusing to look at him while giving him sparse details of her breakup with Jerry. "I agreed to go on one blind date planned by each of my housemates. They assume I'm depressed, and this is supposed to get me back into the dating game. I am *not* depressed and have no desire to get back into the dating game. This is only to get them off my back."

"I find it difficult to believe that you were jilted." He placed one hand on top of hers.

"Don't feel sorry for me." She snatched her hand away, making two fists, and tapping the table lightly. "After discovering his idea to marry me and have two - - not one, mind you, but two - - other women on the side, I dared him to come around again."

"Ah. So I'm the third blind date."

"The last blind date."

"I see." He pushed his chair back and excused himself to make a telephone call.

Tilting her head, she watched him walk away and murmured, "He looks as good going as he does coming. Wonder why Debbie didn't keep this one for herself?"

The man returned to the table just as the server came for their order. Francine realized they'd been so busy talking that neither one had looked at the menu.

"I'll choose for us." He ordered steak, potatoes and house salad. "That should make it simple enough."

"This wine is divine." Francine took another sip. Having been so engrossed in their conversation, the server who'd kept her glass filled, had become invisible.

"Glad you like it. By the way, do you have to grade these three dates?"

"That's the fun of it." She waved her finger in the air. "Shouldn't be telling you that part."

"I'm curious. How do I rate so far?"

Francine was beginning to mellow and couldn't keep herself from responding, "You're way ahead of the curve, what with the car and this restaurant."

"But I have that thing about being late."

"Right, but the good points might just outweigh the bad." She lifted her glass and emptied its contents. A warm feeling was spreading throughout her body, and her face felt flushed. "From the alcohol or the company?"

Once again, the server came to refill her glass. The wine was having an obvious effect on her. Jackson stayed her hand. "Better wait until the food arrives before you sip anymore."

His touch sent a gazillion tingles up her arm. Francine was sure they were the same kind a person experienced just prior to a heart attack.

They laughed and chatted about their work. He gave vague details about himself, and Francine was oblivious to the fact that he kept guiding the conversation back to her.

She shared more information than normal with someone she'd just met. She told him that two of her housemates, Lillie and Marcie, were employees at the secretarial service that Francine now owned and operated. The previous owner, Mrs. Casey, had trained her well, and at her retirement, had made Francine an acceptable offer to purchase the business. She enjoyed the work and the independence. Her responsibilities of ownership had proven more exciting and challenging than overwhelming.

When the time came to leave, Jackson placed his arm around her waist to steady her.

She leaned into the curve of his arm as they waited for the

young man to bring the car around. "The food made four good points for you." She told him.

"Oh? What was the third one? I don't remember you saying."

"I'll tell you later." *Hiccups go away.*

Jackson helped her to get into the car and asked, "Where do you live?"

"With Debbie." Her words were beginning to slur.

"I don't know where Debbie lives."

"You must not know Debbie very well."

He didn't answer and the two were quiet for the ride, except for Francine's giving directions.

"I'll walk you to the door." Against her protests, Jackson continued to hold her about the waist. "Did this date include a goodnight kiss?"

Francine tilted her head upward, but staggered backward. "I don't remember."

Catching her, he pulled her close.

She melded into his hard body, trying to deal with his hands, while he did magic with her lips. Francine realized that the soft moan had come from her.

He propped her against the door and touched his finger to the tip of her nose, and jamming his hands into his pants pockets, skipped down the steps. She heard him whistling. Francine continued to watch as he got to his car. Turning to look at her, he touched two fingers to his temple in a salute. The door behind her came open, and she crashed to the floor where she lay staring upward into Debbie's face.

"Where have you been?"

"With Mark. You win. He's perfect."

"I win what?" Debbie's nostrils flared. "Mark had a flat tire. By the time he got there, you'd gone. I repeat, where were you?"

Lillie and Marcie arrived from upstairs and helped Francine to her feet and into the kitchen. "What's going on?" Marcie asked.

"I'm trying to find out where she's been, but she's drunk."

Marcie asked. "How much have you had to drink? Where were you?"

"With Mark." Francine insisted.

"Don't give us that." Debbie said. "I'm telling you that by the time Mark arrived, you were gone."

Francine stretched her eyes trying to focus. "Oh no, get me ice water."

Debbie brought a glass of ice water to Francine and slapped a wet cloth across her forehead with obvious anger.

"Who were you with, Francine?"

"Mark. Or, at least I thought it was Mark."

"You went with someone who got you drunk, and you don't even know who he is?" Debbie's tone was furious. "You could've been with the Boston strangler."

"Is he still alive?" Lillie asked.

"Don't be stupid, Lillie." Debbie said. "This is important." Turning back to Francine, she demanded, "Start from the beginning."

Francine related the events of the evening. "I thought the man was Mark, and he never told me anything different. I waited at Joe's, and the man was thirty-five minutes late, but he never corrected me." The world and everything in it dissolved into the background as reality brought her back to soberness. "You mean I was with a perfect stranger?"

Debbie crossed the room to the telephone and dialed the number for Joe's Bar and Grill.

"What? That was who?" Replacing the telephone, Debbie turned to face the others.

"Well?" They asked in unison.

"Joe says that Jackson Tanner came into the bar and tried to order a beer, but you chewed him out for being late and then demanded the two of you leave. You were with Jackson Tanner."

"Who is Jackson Tanner?" Marcie asked.

"The most eligible bachelor in town *and* his family happen

to own the Molly Building, *and* Francine happens to rent office space from their corporation."

"I'm going to be sick." Francine turned pale and held out her arms.

"I guess you are." Debbie crossed her arms, glaring at Francine.

"Really. I'm going to be sick." The other girls scrambled to get her to her feet and to the bathroom. Francine slid to her knees, and in an ungraceful manner, lost all of her fine supper.

An hour and several cups of black coffee later, Francine announced, "I'm going to kill him."

"When?" asked a naive Lillie.

"Tomorrow. I'm going to kill him tomorrow. Too sick to kill him tonight. Where does he live?"

"We can find out." Lillie said in a hopeful voice.

"You want to find out where he lives, Lillie, so she can kill him?" Marcie said.

"No, I guess not."

"There's nothing we can do tonight." Debbie offered, "Let's get you to bed, so you can sleep off this stupidity. Why did you keep drinking? You seldom drink."

"I don't know. The glass was never empty, and he was so handsome and gracious. The food was wonderful, and the music romantic."

"Hey, a goodnight kiss was not part of the bargain. Did you let Jackson kiss you?" Debbie asked.

"No. He kissed me, but . . ."

"But, you didn't let him?"

"Yes, I let him. No, I let Mark. I thought it was Mark."

"How did he kiss?" Lillie was giggling.

"It was, well . . . experienced."

"Well . . .?" Again, the others spoke in unison.

"Perfect."

Chapter 2

I t was late morning before Francine pulled herself together, searched the listings in the phone book and located the address for Jackson Tanner. At one-thirty P.M., she drove up the long, circular driveway and rang the doorbell. It was an elegant, country-style home overlooking a large lake. Columns on the front porch reached to the second story porch.

"Hello. May I help you?" The woman who answered the door was blond-haired, petite, drop dead gorgeous and introduced herself as "Brenda Tanner." Francine's courage wavered. She drew a deep breath and renewed her determination. She would make sure that Jackson Tanner didn't think she was anything other than a respectable businesswoman.

"I, uh, need to speak to your husband." Francine added, "Please?"

"Sorry. My husband is in France."

"France?"

"Yes. He's in the Air Force on assignment there."

"Your husband is Jackson Tanner, isn't he?"

"Nooo. My husband, Travis, and Jackson Tanner are brothers. Jackson is here though. And, you are?"

"I'm Francine Bruckner."

"Francine." The woman beamed as if expecting her and said, "I'm glad to meet you. Come in, and I'll get Jackson."

Jackson emerged from around the corner, "Right here. Hi, Francine."

At that moment, a curly-haired blond princess came bounding down the hallway. "Oh, Daddy, she did come, and you said you didn't invite her to the party."

"Party?" Francine looked from Jackson to the little girl and then to Brenda.

"Well, I didn't think she would come. Now she's here. Isn't that grand?"

"Grand?" Francine was confused.

"Come on, Francine, we're swimming before we eat."

"Swimming?"

"Should you be repeating everything like that?" Whispering, he leaned close to her cheek and mimicked her words of the previous evening.

Francine turned to him. "I need to speak to you in private."

"Can it please wait?" He asked. "My daughter, Meagan, is ten today, and she has guests."

"Come on, Francine, let's have a swim, then we can eat hot dogs and cake and ice cream." Meagan reached for her hand.

The face of the little girl was touching. "I don't have a swimsuit. I'll watch."

"Can't she wear one of Mum's suits?" The little girl turned toward her daddy.

"Sure she can, Honey. I believe you can find one just the right size. Take her on up. Go with them, Brenda."

"Come on, we'll get you fixed up." Brenda was still smiling as she took Francine's hand and pulled her towards the stairs.

"Have I stepped into a parallel universe?" She looked back and saw Jackson leaning against the doorway, with one arm propped into the bend of the other, chin resting on his fist.

When they reached the top of the stairs, Meagan grabbed Francine's other hand, and she and Brenda pulled her into a bedroom.

"Where's your Mother, Meagan?"

"In heaven."

"Just a minute, Brenda. You'll have to clue me in here. What's going on? You seem to be in on the joke. I'm not swimming, by the way."

Brenda pushed Meagan toward the door. "You go on and see about your other guests. I'll help Francine find the right suit."

"But, she's my guest." Meagan said.

"We'll be right there, I promise." Brenda closed the door behind her. "Jackson told me about your mixed-up date last evening. He figured that it was a mistaken identity, but thought you were delightful and intriguing. He'd been working on a merger all day, and well, you were a surprising diversion."

"He knew I had mistaken him for someone else all along? He thinks I'm delightful, and I'm humiliated. He should've told me he wasn't my date. I came over here to kill him for tricking me," and she continued, "to further humiliate me, he's told you all about it, and you find it amusing as well."

"There's no need to be humiliated, really. He didn't know what to do at first. Then, curiosity led him into going along with it. I've never known him to be that daring. You were alluring from the description he gave me. He described you as someone with snapping brown eyes, gorgeous black hair and a model's body." Brenda kept talking as she pointed to the privacy screen for Francine to use. She handed Francine a simple black and red two-piece bathing suit.

"Hmmm." Francine grunted in disbelief.

"I can't wear this." Francine came around the screen and stared at herself in the mirror. "This is much too revealing. Besides, I don't wear bikinis. Don't you have something else?"

Brenda laughed. "Nonsense. It's a great fit, and you do fill it in much better than Jackson's wife did."

"This doesn't feel right. Get me out of this, please? I promise

I won't kill him, and you'll never hear from me again. I'll slip out of the door unnoticed."

"Not on your life. Jackson might *kill me* if I messed up his chance for a second date with you, and Meagan would be crushed if you disappointed her on her birthday." Brenda's eyes twinkled as she tossed Francine a large towel. "Use this."

"You love every minute of this, don't you? I doubt he'd care for a second date with an idiot."

"Take my word for it. He does not think you're an idiot. He had a wonderful time. We've been trying to get Jackson to go out with someone for the past three years, and you worked magic in one night."

"Yeah, and he thinks I'm a big joke."

"I can promise you that's not true, so relax. Follow me. We have a party to attend."

Taking a deep breath, and pulling the large towel about her, Francine followed the woman downstairs. Brenda's sweetness and ability to keep the conversation flowing helped to calm Francine. They joined Meagan and her three cousins and several other children for a swim. No other Moms were in sight, taking advantage of free time, no doubt.

After deciding she'd stayed long enough to be courteous, she announced that she was going to change her clothes.

"It's time to eat now. You must try one of my magnificent hot dogs. Have a seat and you shall have the first one." Jackson was in front of her with a platter of grilled wieners.

As she dried herself, she noticed Jackson was gazing at her. Wrapping the towel about her body again, she eased into the chair and prepared a hot dog, which she ate, along with a helping of pasta salad.

Jackson sat beside her and filled his plate. "Am I forgiven?"

"I came here to seek revenge." She couldn't resist his smile and manner. Her heart did a flip-flop, and she decided then and there she could never be angry with him again.

"And, what did this revenge entail?" He tilted his head to one side.

"A slow, agonizing death." Francine blushed as she remembered that Brenda was looking on.

"Sounds interesting."

She picked up her glass of soda just as Meagan rushed over to them.

"Did you ask her yet, Dad?"

"No, I thought I'd leave that to you. You ask her."

"Ask me what, Darling?" Francine placed her drink on the table and leaned over to face Meagan.

"I need a Mommy."

Shocked, Francine jerked backwards waving her hand, and knocked over the glass and spilled the drink all over her. She jumped to her feet as the towel fell away.

Jackson responded by snatching the towel and blotting her chest and stomach with it.

"If you don't mind." Francine grabbed his hand and pushed it away. Again, electric sparks shot up her arm attacking her heart.

"Sorry. Trying to help." From the look on his face, he was having the same reaction.

He held up both hands and backed away. "Don't be alarmed. It's not as drastic as Meagan makes it sound. Hear her out."

Meagan, unaware of the chemistry between the two, continued, "We're having a mother and daughter supper at church Friday, and I need a Mother. My youth director said it could be a friend, or my father's girlfriend, so I thought you could go with me."

"That's all?" Francine stared down at the little girl and smiled.

Jackson leaned over and whispered in her ear. "Unless you want more?"

"I want revenge. I deserve revenge." Francine was embarrassed. "Why not take your aunt?"

"Aunt Brenda can't take me. She already has three daughters.

Besides, I want my own Mommy, even if it is pretend. Just this once, please."

All eyes were on her, and Francine surmised what a criminal felt while being questioned under a hot light. "I guess so. Of course, I'll go. What time shall I come for you?"

After hearing the details of the pretend mom thing from Brenda and Meagan, she decided it was time to leave. "Thanks for everything. I enjoyed the party, but I need to change now and go home." She turned, hoping to see her jousting partner once again, but he'd disappeared.

Francine later told her housemates about the afternoon and about her plans for Friday evening.

"You're going to do what?" Debbie asked, not at all pleased with this turn of events.

"You were supposed to kill him." Lillie reminded her.

"Don't let him kiss you again, not like before." Marcie warned.

"I'm not going to let him kiss me. He won't be there. I'm going to be a baby-sitter that night for his little girl. That's all."

"Can't believe he went home and told his sister-in-law and his little girl about your date, or that you would go along with this hair-brained idea. I'm starting to question your sanity, Francine." Debbie shook her head.

"*I'm* starting to question my sanity. However, you have yourself to thank for this mess. It's doubtful that he told his sister-in-law everything. You don't think he did, do you?"

"Me to thank?"

"Of course. If I hadn't been waiting on your Mark, and if he'd not been late, I wouldn't be in this mess."

"Blame yourself for jumping to conclusions, and you still owe Mark a date."

"No way. One disaster is enough, besides . . ."

"Uh huh. You don't seem to be depressed about Jerry anymore. Maybe our plan worked and you're cured." Lillie offered.

"Cured for sure." Francine nodded in agreement and left the room.

Debbie had a worried look on her face and murmured, "It will be a slow and agonizing ordeal for Mr. Jackson Tanner if this rich boy hurts my best friend."

Determined to have the last word before she rushed up the stairs, Francine called back over her shoulder, "Your fault."

Chapter 3

Francine parked her van in front of the Tanner residence unprepared for the exuberant welcome from Meagan or the hurried goodbye from Jackson Tanner. She checked her make-up, patted her hair and turned from her rearview mirror as Jackson tossed back to her a few remarks.

"Hi, Francine. Thanks. Hope you two have a great time. Gotta go, I'm late." He was dressed in a deep blue tuxedo with curls bobbing across his forehead and headed toward a long, black limousine. Francine watched with her eyes bulging and her mouth gaped wide until she felt Meagan tugging at her jacket.

"Hi, Francine. Dad said we could use the Jaguar, but please, please, please, let's go in that neat van. Will you fix my hair and tie my sash? I hate Mary Jane stockings; will you not tell Dad if I wear my knee socks? What time is it? Don't just stare. We hav'ta hurry." Meagan grabbed Francine's hand and snatched her to attention.

"Yes and Yes, Yes. No. Seven-fifteen. Now where is your brush?" Francine answered the questions in what she thought was perfect succession, causing the child to bend over giggling. The two hurried inside to complete the job of getting Meagan ready. Francine understood the Mary Jane stocking thing. They're milk white and have no appeal whatsoever. Most of the time, they end up sagging around the ankles after about five minutes of being worn. She agreed with Meagan that they were much too childish for a ten-year-old and in her opinion, ugly. Soon, Meagan was dressed to their satisfaction, tucked into the van and on the way to First Trinity Baptist Church. They parked in front of a small building and saw several women directing cars. Francine took a big breath and walked toward the group. Meagan introduced Francine to five teachers and several other young ladies as "my mother." Then she was off to find their name cards, leaving Francine with the teachers, drained of color and at a loss for words. Things were moving too fast and in the wrong direction.

"It's so nice to meet you," the teachers said almost in unison, eyeing her from head to toe.

"Wait a minute. I'm not really her mother." She gave a faint smile. Before she could explain further, the teacher, introduced as Mrs. Butler, stopped her with a wave of her hand.

"That's all right. It's nice to know that a man's girlfriend and child get along so well. When you're married, you'll have a great relationship."

"But, we aren't getting married." She wondered what in the world Meagan had told these people.

"Oh?" Mrs. Butler raised her eyebrows and turned to lead everyone inside, leaving Francine speechless. She had no alternative than to follow.

The speaker who stood at the podium pounded the gavel. The room became quiet. "It's time to say the blessing. Will everyone find your seats?"

Francine sighed and crossed to the table where Meagan stood beaming. She shook her head at the girl and frowned. Meagan smiled and pretended not to notice.

The evening had been well planned, and everyone seemed to be having a great time, but there was never an opportunity to explain her position to the teachers. They called the name, Francine Tanner, for the grand door prize, which was a day long total make over and massage. With a quick burn to her cheeks, Francine snatched her head to face Meagan. The child refused to look at her as everyone applauded.

Meagan hurried from the table saying, "I'll get the ticket for you."

Although the evening was fun, Francine couldn't relax and in her mind, cursed Jackson Tanner, Mark, and her three friends.

When they arrived home, Francine went inside with Meagan, hoping Jackson was at home to discuss the situation. They found him sitting at the kitchen table drinking coffee. He was in his tuxedo, minus the cumber bund, tie and shoes. He still made a striking and distracting picture. She tried to focus on what she needed to say.

She squeaked out the words, "We have to talk."

Jackson's stocking feet had been propped in another chair but he dropped them to the floor and gave her his full attention. With his head tilted back, he amazed her again with the greenest eyes she'd ever seen.

Meagan rushed over, gave him a quick kiss and hug. "Night Daddy. Why not give Francine some coffee? She was great. She won the best door prize." Then Meagan was out of sight but not out of mind.

He must have noticed Francine's frown because he asked, "Is something wrong?" Standing, he walked to the cabinet and reached for a mug, motioning her toward a chair. "Have a seat. Take anything in your coffee?"

"No. Listen to me, will you?" Her voice was louder, and she remained standing.

He gave her a startled look. Jackson poured the coffee and sat the mug on the table near where she stood and said, "I'm listening. Go ahead."

"Your daughter introduced me as her mother."

"So? It was a mother-daughter function. I thought you

understood that. You were filling in. Meagan was only trying to make you feel comfortable."

"Meagan was *not* trying to make me feel comfortable! I'm not her mother, and my name is not Francine Tanner."

"Well, it was just for tonight. She had to take someone. You were her choice, and I certainly agreed it was safe. After all, I didn't think you were the type to kidnap her for ransom."

"Safe? That's what I am? Safe? This is not a joke, Jackson."

"Sure, you seem like a nice person, one with whom I could trust my only child."

"When I tried to explain to, uh, the teachers, Sunday school teachers at that, they thought I was your live-in girlfriend."

"Why on earth would they think that?" He gave a nonchalant lift to his shoulders.

"I told them we weren't married."

"And?"

"And, they thought I was your girlfriend. Then the meeting started, and I wasn't able to explain that we aren't even dating."

"We've had one date." Jackson offered another slow, tantalizing grin.

"Do you understand that these people think I'm uh . . ." She stopped at his grin, stomped her foot and with hands on her hips, continued, "You think this is funny."

He hesitated before speaking. Staring at her and moving his eyes over her body, he gave a shake of his head and shoulders, as if dismissing the apparent electricity between them. "Not funny, Francine, but quite amusing. I can live with their opinions, and Meagan doesn't appear to have a problem with it."

"I have a problem with it."

"What, a problem with not living me?"

"No. I have a problem with their opinions."

"All right. Have your coffee. I'll get it straightened out tomorrow."

"Promise?"

"Would I lie?" There was a twinkle in his eyes.

"Maybe not, but you are pretty quiet about the truth."

Both heads turned at a noise at the door.

"Meagan, come on in." Jackson called to his daughter who had been listening to the conversation.

"Am I in trouble?"

"Not with me, but you have something to say to Francine, don't you?"

"Yes sir. I'm sorry, Francine. Even my best friend has a stepmother, why couldn't I pretend for just one night?"

"Meagan, that's not the problem. You led those people to believe that I was your new mother. Then when I tried to correct that, they believed I was your daddy's girlfriend, and that I lived in this house. That didn't leave them with a very good impression of me, now did it?"

"I'm sorry. I'll tell them Sunday."

"Your dad promised tomorrow." Francine eyed the child then turned to face Jackson.

He shrugged. "Sunday's only a couple days away."

She turned to Meagan who said, "I promise. Would you come with me?"

"To Sunday School?"

"Yes, you do go to Sunday School, don't you?"

"I used to go."

"Will you come early enough to fix my hair and help with my dress? Can we ride in that neat van? Daddy will you ride with us? I have to go to bed now. See you Sunday." She waved and was gone again.

Francine clicked her tongue against her teeth in frustration and turned to see Jackson doubled over in laughter. "You really do think this is funny, don't you? I'm getting nowhere here. She creates a new problem every time she promises to remedy another. You need to learn how to discipline your daughter."

Mumbling to herself, she headed to the door.

Jackson rose so fast that he almost slipped in his stocking feet. "I know. I let her get by with too much to compensate for losing her mother. Let me walk you to your car." He hurried behind her without his shoes. Jackson opened the door to her van.

Before Francine could get into the van, she turned to ask, "Are you going with her Sunday to get this mess straightened out?" He was so close she caught the smell of coffee on his breath and the fragrance of aftershave that teased her senses.

"Sure I will. Here, let me help you."

"I am capable of getting in by myself, thank you."

He reached for her and wrapped both arms about her waist, then slid them upward until her arms were propped on his shoulders.

"Not this again," she whispered, attempting to squirm away from the intimacy, which didn't help matters.

Jackson's lips brushed hers, and his kiss deepened before he made an abrupt step backwards, touched his finger to the tip of her nose and whispered, "Goodnight."

Francine was glad that the vehicle door was open. Her legs would not have held her upright had she not been able to grab the door handle and support herself as she climbed onto the seat.

Glancing back, she saw Jackson watching from the porch. He touched his hand to his forehead in that mock salute.

She was still muttering when she entered the kitchen at home where her housemates sat drinking coffee. "I do have to kill him, but I don't know when or how. It has to be soon." She was angry and poured the hot liquid in her cup a little too fast, sloshing it over her hand.

"Confound that man." Francine shook her hand to cool the pain as the other three girls stared with perplexed looks.

Marcie moved to hand her wet paper towels and Debbie broke the silence. "What's he done now, sprung a couple more kids on you?" They giggled -- Francine glared.

"He kissed me again."

"Some problem," Lillie said. "The only bad thing about his kisses is that you're so weak in the knees afterwards you can't stand."

"And, he knows it. How can he claim to be a man sworn off of women and kiss like that?"

"How do you know he's sworn off women?" Debbie asked.

"That's the rumor in the building that I heard before I met him. Loved his late wife so much, no one can take her place. According to his sister-in-law, *his* friends have been trying to fix him up with dates, like somebody else's friends I know."

"Here, Francine." Marcie had replaced the spilled coffee and sat the mug in front of her.

"Sounds like you have yourself quite a man there." Debbie said. "How's that hand?"

"He's not my man. All I have is an unpaid baby-sitting job. My hand is fine."

"Maybe the kiss is payment enough, huh?" Lillie asked.

Francine gave a slanted look toward Lillie and Debbie that said, "back off."

The look had no effect on Lillie who asked, "When you gonna see 'im again?"

"What is this – twenty questions?" Francine dipped her head downward as she lifted the cup with caution. "Supposed to see him Sunday at Sunday school." She barely whispered the last part.

"That's nice." The other three pressed their lips together, remaining poker faced.

"I *am not* going to Sunday School with them. Meagan is supposed to tell those women that I'm just a friend filling in so she'd have someone with her that night. She can't be trusted and will do something to humiliate me. I know she will."

"Why not go anyway? She's only ten. You're the grown-up. Don't tell me you're afraid of a little girl?" Marcie asked.

"If she doesn't think of a way to embarrass me, Jackson will.

I believe this is a contest for them to see who can get the bigger rise out of me."

"Whatcha gonna wear?" Lillie asked.

"Drat!" Francine stood, taking her mug to the sink to rinse before shoving it into the dishwasher. She stormed from the room.

Despite her adamant vow not to go to the church with Jackson and Meagan, she spent the next afternoon trying on dresses. Francine continued to toss them aside before deciding on a pale yellow two-piece suit and beige sandals.

After supper, to avoid further teasing, Francine went to her room early. Alone with her thoughts, she argued with herself, trying to rational the situation. "This is what I've tried to avoid." Not that he was interested in a relationship, but she was afraid of her emotions that he evoked. Tossing about in restless sleep, she dozed off about three A.M. The alarm was easy to tune out the next morning, but it was impossible to ignore the jolt that almost bounced her to the floor. Meagan had vaulted into the room and onto the bed.

"Where did you come from, and what are you doing here?"

"Get up, sleepy head." Meagan pulled at the covers. "Dad's taking us to breakfast before Sunday School."

After getting over the shock of having her peace burglarized and an uninvited guest in her house, she whined, "I'm not going. I don't feel well."

"Oh yes you are." The masculine voice belonged to the hunk standing in the doorway with arms folded across his chest. "I'm not going to face the Teacher Brigade by myself."

"What are you doing in my house? What are you doing in my bedroom?" She screamed, ducking her head beneath the covers, thinking, "This must be hades. Me with no make-up and my hair in a tumbled mess."

Meagan tugged at the covers. "He can't see anything silly."

"I asked if you were decent. The girls said you were." Jackson offered.

"Go away. I'm sick." She could see her three housemates standing behind Jackson each giving innocent shrugs. "I'll get you conspirators later."

"Whatever is wrong with you'll be better once you've showered and dressed." Jackson continued. "Besides, we promised to get this mess straightened out today, and I won't do that if you aren't with us."

"Please?" Meagan purred in the sweetest voice.

She was getting warmer by the minute and knew it was not because of the covers. "Get out!"

"Me?" Meagan's voice wavered.

"Not you. Him." She peeked from beneath the covers and pointed at Jackson.

"All right. I'll wait downstairs. Hurry, I'm starved."

When they sat in the restaurant, she realized how famished she was and dug into the bacon, eggs and grits from the breakfast bar. Not long afterwards, they walked up the pavement to the little red brick Sunday school building next to the main church building. It was then she did feel sick. Bracing herself, she followed the other two hoping to gain some of their apparent confidence.

Mrs. Butler smiled when she spied Jackson. He walked over to her and said, "Good morning. Here we are."

"I'm so happy to see you." A frown and wrinkled forehead replaced her smile when she looked at Francine.

Jackson continued, "Mrs. Butler, Meagan has something to tell you."

"Later Daddy, there's Janet." And, off she ran.

"You tell her!" Francine demanded.

"Mrs. Butler. I believe Meagan gave you a false impression about my and Francine's relationship. She had her heart set on having someone with her at the mother-daughter banquet, and Francine was gracious enough to attend with her. She and I are just . . ."

"Dating." Meagan shouted as she and Janet ran past them into the building. The bell rang, and Mrs. Butler left them to greet other people. Jackson took Francine's elbow to usher her inside.

"Close your mouth, Francine. It's not the end of the world, you know." His comment was terse.

On the ride home, silence reigned until Francine spoke. "Jackson, this didn't work out as we planned. I'll leave the matter to you since I will *never* see those ladies again."

Francine refused to look at Meagan, who was humming and staring out the window. Jackson glared straight ahead, not answering. His anger showed in the way he kept clenching his jaw. Francine decided it would be best to remain quiet.

Jackson was curt when he said goodbye to her. "I will talk with you soon."

She watched as they drove away and guessed that he was giving his daughter a tongue-lashing, because she saw that her head was facing downward.

Three weeks passed, and there was no word from Jackson or Meagan.

"Don't ask me again." Francine instructed her housemates. She wouldn't admit it to them, but she was now more depressed than ever and convinced that her earlier decision not to get involved again had been the right one. If she ever decided to attend church again, it would be across town and a different denomination.

By Thursday afternoon, she'd decided on a mini-vacation to the beach, alone. She made reservations and planned to retreat from the world with a couple of good books. With her bags packed and in the van, she could leave from work and was mentally already on her way.

"The phone's for you, Francine. Think you need to take this one. It's something about Meagan." Marcie held her hand over the phone.

With an "oh no" expression, she listened to the caller. "I'm sorry she's sick, but shouldn't you call her father?"

The voice on the other end of the line informed her that Meagan's father was out of town, and Meagan had instructed her to call this number instead.

"Well, what about her aunt or grandparents? Her grandfather works in this building. The family owns the building where I am."

The voice informed her that Jackson Tanner, Sr. and his wife were also out of town. "I believe it's real this time. She has a temperature. Meagan has pretended to be sick so many times before that the aunt won't come for her again. We can't keep her here with the other children. She may need her pediatrician."

"Why aren't you telling this to her aunt or Mr. Tanner's secretary?"

"We did. They were fine with our calling you, and you're wasting precious time."

"Oh great. All right, tell me how to get to the school." Francine scratched directions onto the notepad. She explained to Marcie and Lillie and hurried out the door. "See you Monday. Guess I'm going to school first, to pick up a sick child."

One of the girls called after her, "Call us, and let us know how Meagan is."

She made a quick trip to the top floor suite of offices to inquire about the Tanners' whereabouts. Mr. Tanner, Sr. was there giving instructions to his secretary. She could only assume they'd lied to the school.

"Excuse me, Mr. Tanner. I'm Francine . . ."

"So, you're Francine. It's so nice to meet you. Sorry I don't have time to chat right now. I have to meet my wife at the airport. We're flying to Cape Cod for the weekend."

"I didn't come to chat. Meagan's school called, and she's sick and needs to be picked up."

"Oh no." He glanced at his watch, either pretending that he was truly too late to pick her up, or that he didn't even know about it.

At any rate, Francine knew the man was aware the school had called.

While she pondered the situation, Mr. Tanner, Sr. continued, "Francine, I hate to ask you, but could you pick her up? She does this about once a month, and I really have to catch that plane. Besides, Jackson will be happier knowing that she's with you."

"What? Where is Jackson? The teacher said she may need her pediatrician."

"Oh, I doubt that, she was fine this morning. She really does this about once a month. Meagan knew we were going out of town and couldn't take her with us this time. It's just a ploy. Believe me. Look, Jackson should be home soon. Nancy here will get word for him to contact you right away. You just pick her up, and I'll see that you're compensated."

"But . . ."

"Gotta go now, really."

Nancy smiled, "She really does this about once a month."

"Can't you pick her up? She's not my child."

"Not mine either." Nancy said. "Besides, Jackson will be calling here soon and would have a fit if nobody was here manning the phones."

Twenty minutes later, she pulled her van into the schoolyard and hurried toward the front door. There was a young woman waiting for her, motioning her to hurry. "She does have a temperature, and a stomach ache. Her pediatrician will meet you at the hospital."

"Oh no." When they reached the nurse's office, she found a pale Meagan, with tears rolling down her cheeks. She lay on the sofa holding her stomach.

Francine lifted the child with the help of her teacher and carried her to the van. "Don't worry, Honey. We'll have you there in no time flat."

"It's her appendix." The doctor told Francine. "We'll have to do surgery."

"When?"

"Now!"

"But, I'm not her mother. You can't do surgery without permission."

"We've got to have somebody's permission and right now."

"Oh no, where's a phone? Quick!" Francine turned away from the doctor and crashed into Jackson's hard chest. "Thank goodness, you're here. They need your permission, now."

"Hi Jackson. It's her appendix, here are the forms, and we have to operate now. Gotta go." The doctor hurried away. Jackson scribbled his name on the form where the girl pointed and rushed down the hall after the doctor.

Francine stared at Jackson's back and heard him say, "I have to see her."

"Come on, but only a second."

A nurse tapped Francine on the shoulder, "Ma'am. Come this way, you can have a seat in the waiting room. There's coffee." She was ushered into a small room with two windows. There was a television in the corner with a picture, but the sound had been lowered. Several other people were there and had pulled their chairs close together. They spoke in soft tones.

Not until she sank into the end of the empty sofa did she realize how weak her legs were. Pressing her hands to her face, she prayed.

"Francine." Hearing Jackson's voice, she raised her tear-stained face. He'd kneeled in front of her and taking her hands, whispered, "Thank you. Thank you."

"She will be all right? I wasted so much time, going up to see your dad and . . ."

"Shh. It's not your fault at all. I'm just thankful that you got to her. The doctor thinks she will be fine. I talked to Nancy at the office after the plane landed. She told me what had happened, and I came straight here."

"What if you hadn't made it? I would have signed that form, you know. What if I had signed it and something had gone wrong?"

"I signed it, Francine. Something may still go wrong."

"But you're her father, and you love her?"

"Don't you love her?"

"What a question. Yes, I love her. I love her."

"She's quite the little frustrating thing, I'll admit." He forced a smile.

"I think even Meagan would agree." She smiled.

"Let me get you a cup of coffee."

"No, Jackson, you sit here. I'll get it for you. You must be exhausted. What a scene to come home to."

"Well, this won't be happening again, or at least not like it has the past three months."

"Why? What's been happening? Sorry, not my business." Francine wondered if there was some romantic involvement, and that would be quite none of her business.

"No, I mean, yes, it's all right that you ask. I've been working on a merger with another company that owns interests in several small airports. This is only one area of Tanner Enterprises but an important one. Today was the clincher, and Mother and Dad were flying out for a celebration weekend. We've all been so tied up with this. That's why. . ." He broke it off.

"She needs a mother, doesn't she?" Francine was surprised to hear herself say the words.

"Yes, are you applying for the job?" She could see he was trying for light banter.

"No. She doesn't need you to hire a mother for her. She needs a real full time mother."

"Well, that wasn't . . ." The doctor entered the room before Jackson finished the sentence.

"She's fine, Jackson. This lady got her here just in time. It'll be a little while. Why don't you two go on home and come back in a couple of hours? She'll be in recovery for a while, and then we'll get her set up in a room."

"All right." He shook the doctor's hand and turned to Francine. "Would you ride with me, Francine? I need to go home and change before coming back."

"I have my van." There was no need to explain ruined weekend plans.

"I'll drop you off first, pick you up later. I plan to stay the night with her, and you will have your van here to drive home. I'm sure she'll be happy for a short visit from you when she wakes up. Please?"

"Sure." Francine followed him to the car. She listened as he talked about the merger before his conversation shifted to Meagan and her anxiety over the loss of her mother and his belief that all these fantasies were her way of filling the void.

He surprised her by asking if she would consider staying the evening with them. Francine was more surprised that she agreed.

At home, she showered and pulled on a pair of jeans and a blue western style shirt.

Debbie, Marcie and Lillie sprawled across her bed plying her with questions, which she answered with only slight patience. "I'm going for a couple hours."

Lillie smiled. "Haven't seen you wear those jeans in a long time, or that shirt. The color shows off your eyes."

"Your minds are working overtime, ladies. Now get out of here. The man has his little girl on his mind, not romance. For that matter, same goes for me." She could say the words aloud, but couldn't deny the growing attraction she felt. "Make yourselves useful and cancel my reservations."

Marcie rushed from the room calling over her shoulder. "I have just the thing for you. It may get a bit chilly in the hospital room. Sometimes, it does." In no time, she was back with a soft blue sweater.

Francine looked back at her three best friends. They stood

with arms about each other, waving. They were the closest things to sisters she had. On impulse, she turned and ran back to them for a hug. The idea flashed through her mind that there would be nothing cool about that hospital room tonight.

Chapter 4

It had been her intention to wait until Meagan woke, speak to her briefly and then leave. Jackson and Meagan begged her to stay. She knew the child would be fine with nurses in and out, but her frightened expression tugged at Francine's heart. Another certainty was that the next afternoon she would spend in the chiropractor's office, getting an adjustment from sitting in that chair all night. She agreed to stay, though this was not her idea of a great evening. Knowing the man was exhausted, she insisted Jackson stretch out on the reclining chair furnished by the hospital. Hindsight told her that she should have suggested they take turns. Each time she dozed, a different nurse would come into the room and flip on the light to check on Meagan. The interruptions didn't bother either Jackson or Meagan, and his snoring was just loud enough to be irritating. He didn't wake up the entire night, and a sleepy Meagan only smiled at the nurses when they checked in. Francine wondered if there might be some unspoken agreement between the nurses. Each time one of them left the room, they neglected to turn the light off or shut the door and acted as if it was broad daylight outside. They would call to other nurses with no concern that the patients or their caregivers were trying to sleep. At least some of them slept.

Being that close to Jackson could have been a wonderful experience under different circumstances. Fearing he would ask her to spend another night there, it was with great relief and thanks giving that she learned they would dismiss Meagan from the hospital later in the day. Francine heard the doctor give Jackson the name of a competent nurse who would stay with the child for several days.

"I don't understand why Francine can't stay with me."

Her eyes stretched wide open but Jackson nixed the idea, "Honey, you know that she has worked all week. Now, she has been kind enough to stay here and sit in that chair all night. We can't impose anymore."

She gave the child a cheerful smile and a hug and promised to check on her soon.

The pain in her neck was slight in the beginning, but as she eased into the van, her body let her know this wouldn't be a short-lived condition. The stiffness in her neck made it difficult for Francine to drive since she had to turn her entire upper torso to look in either direction. The other girls met her at the front door, a cup of good strong, black coffee in hand, eager for a report. They were disappointed because all she wanted was a shower and nap. She assured them the romantic rendezvous they'd hoped for did not happen. The hot shower felt wonderful but did little to relieve the pain and stiffness that had increased in her neck and spread downward into her shoulders and spine. Francine didn't attempt to go to work, and lying in bed did nothing to relieve her condition. A nap was out of the question. Standing, walking or sitting upright did nothing to help either.

Lillie came in with an ice pack. "I really don't know where to put it. You're hurting from your neck all the way down your spine."

"I know, but thanks anyway. Guess I know what I'll have to do, but hate the thought of trying to drive to the doctor's office."

"You won't have to drive. We'll get you there." Lillie could be the great little nurse when the situation called for it.

A visit to the chiropractor was inevitable. She asked Lillie to make the call to Dr. Sanders' office. His instructions were to bring her right away. All three girls helped her to Lillie's car, which was easier to get into, rather than her van. They tucked a feather pillow behind her and lowered the back of the seat. After an adjustment, she had a massage and rested on the table for another hour. Francine left the doctor's office feeling much better but $175.00 poorer. A full body ice pack might have been cheaper but an insufficient substitute.

Lillie dropped her off in front of the house and left to park the car. "Now what?" she thought to herself seeing a young boy standing on the steps, holding one box with another at his feet. He was pounding on the door. Seeing her, he gave a relieved smile.

"Can I help you?" The box was small, but she could have sworn it moved in his hands.

"You Francine Bruckner?"

"Yes. Is that package for me?" She peeked inside as the delivery boy shoved the box into her hands. Two tiny eyes stared up at her. "Oh no, you don't. Where did this come from? You wait one cotton pickin' minute. There must be some mistake. I haven't ordered a dog, and I'm not about to keep it. Here, take it back."

"No Ma'am. You said your name is Francine Bruckner, and my instructions were to deliver this package to you. My shift is officially over as of five minutes ago. I got me a hot date. I don't have time to take that dog nowhere. My job is done." With that, he stepped away and bounded down the steps leaving Francine holding the box, with her mouth wide open. No wonder he had such a relieved look on his face when he saw her.

She reached inside the box and pulled the tiny blanket away from the eyes of a longhaired Chihuahua that stared up at her, tongue hanging out. Happy that he was in no immediate danger, the tiny pup gave a soft bark before snuggling back into the blanket.

The door swung open. It was Debbie. "Sorry, did you forget your key? What in the world was all that pounding about?" She lowered her gaze down to the box in Francine's hands.

"It was a delivery boy. I got here just in time for him to give me this."

"Oops, looks like it's time for another house meeting." Debbie called for Marcie who came from upstairs with a towel around her head. Lillie had parked the car and appeared from the kitchen.

"Whatcha got in the box?" Lillie asked.

"Oh, he's so cute, can I hold him?" Marcie reached for the pup.

"It's the cutest little Chihuahua I've ever seen. I didn't know you were getting a dog. What will you name him?" Debbie interjected. "No. I guess it's whatcha gonna name her? Looks like a girl."

They hurled questions at an exasperated Francine.

"Nothing. I'm doing nothing. Hello? You three listen to me. This is not my dog. I am not going to name him or her anything. Don't know where it came from or why."

Francine stood with the box in her hand. Lillie peeked inside and pulled out a card and said, "Look, here's a note."

Francine snatched the note from her hand as the other three girls sat down on the hall floor, motioning for the frowning Francine to join them. Marcie placed the dog in the middle of their circle, but Francine stood as she read aloud.

"Dear Francine. Thank you so much for getting me to the hospital and staying with us. This is my thank-you gift to you. I hope you like it. Come see me as soon as you can. Love Meagan."

"Good grief. This is a thank-you gift from Meagan. Now, why would she do that without asking me? Why would that crazy man allow her to do this without asking me first? Does he ever make that child act sensible? He had to have picked this dog out. Meagan is too sick to have done this on her own. She really does need a mother. He needs a psychiatrist. I need help."

Francine joined the other girls on the floor, and Lillie placed the puppy onto her lap and it promptly wet on her.

"Gee." Debbie said. "He bonded with you."

"It's not a he remember, it's a she." Lillie corrected her.

"What difference does it make? I'm wet. Here take it." Francine shoved the dog into Debbie's hands. Standing, she tried to pull her wet skirt away from her legs.

"How could a little thing like that wet so much?" Lillie asked.

"What are you going to do?" Marcie asked.

"I'm going to change my clothes for starters, then, call Jackson Tanner, give him a piece of my mind and instruct him to come get this dog, pronto. I don't have time for a dog. Besides, I don't have dog food and have no plans to go shopping for any. Don't you have to feed puppies every couple of hours, like a baby?"

"This is like a baby, but I doubt you have to feed him that much. Oh, let's keep him." Marcie pulled the puppy into her arms.

"It's a her, and you keep her if you want. It's not my dog."

"I saw another box on the porch. Wait a minute." Debbie came back and opened it to find food for the puppy. Meagan had thought of everything.

"I want nothing to do with this dog or that entire Tanner bunch of crazy people." Francine threw her hands up and headed up the stairs to change clothes leaving the puppy with her friends.

After dialing the Tanner telephone number a dozen times over the next hour and getting a busy signal, she gave up. It was still daylight outside, but she decided to try for that long awaited nap. She pulled on an ankle-length soft, flannel gown and stretched out on her bed, fluffed her pillows and with a long yawn, sank her head into them. At that point, she didn't know where the dog was and didn't dare ask. She decided not to show any interest whatsoever, at least for now. Let the other girls become attached to it, but not her, no matter how cute. There was a principle involved in this situation somewhere, and she intended to determine what it was -- after a good night's rest.

It took her only seconds to fall asleep, but she woke to the persistent ringing of the doorbell. After calling to the other girls and getting no response, she dragged herself from the bed and hurried down the stairs not taking time to pull on slippers. All was quiet, and none of the others or the dog was in sight.

Opening the door, she found Jackson standing there. "Thank goodness you've come to get that confounded dog. You have to take her back. I don't know what you were thinking."

"What dog, and take it back where?"

She stepped backward and too late felt the oozy, gooey stuff squeeze between her toes. "Oh no!" Francine pulled her gown upward so as not to get the gooey stuff on it, thankful for hardwood floors. "See, this is why I don't want a dog."

"My goodness, where did that come from? Stand still. Here, I'll carry you to the bathroom." He reached for her.

"Oh no you won't. I'm capable of walking by myself." In an attempt to keep her toes in the air, she slouched over trying to walk on her heels, stepping once again in the puppy's accident.

"You keep trying to walk and you'll have this stuff all over the place. Where's the bathroom?"

"There's one at the end of the hall. Believe me, the stuff between my toes is not your problem. The dog is your problem. I'll walk by myself, thank you very much."

"I wouldn't advise it." He grabbed her up, ignoring her protests, and marched down the hall toward the back of the house, shifting her to open the door.

Feeling as if she was about to fall, her arms went about his neck, knowing that her face was too close to his for comfort. So was that nice fresh fragrance he wore.

"That's better." Jackson smiled down at her as he walked into the bathroom. Once inside the room, he attempted to release her so that her foot would go into the commode.

"Don't put my foot in there."

"That's where this stuff goes, Francine." Ignoring her remark, he leaned forward to put her foot into the water. He reached for the handle.

"Don't flush it. My foot's in there."

"I repeat. That's where this stuff goes. Don't worry. Your foot's attached to the rest of you. Petite as you are, I do believe you're too large to go down with the water, but I could do this better if you'd let go of my neck now."

Feeling foolish, she turned loose, tried to stand on the other foot, lost her balance and fell backward. He grabbed her in time. "Here sit."

"Sit where?"

He reached for a towel. "You can remove your foot from the water and sit on the commode. I think that's about all of it. He lowered the lid and knelt before her. I'll dry your foot."

"This is humiliating."

"I didn't know you had a dog. When did you get him?"

"I don't have a dog. Don't you have any idea what your daughter is doing?"

"You have a dog running around doing his business on your floor, and you don't know you have a dog, and you have the nerve to ask me if I know what my daughter is doing?" He was sitting on his heels as he finished drying her foot. "There, that about does it."

"Your daughter sent me that dog as a so called thank-you gift, and it's a she. I've tried to call you for the past two hours so you can come get him."

"It's a her."

"How do you know?"

"You just told me. Francine, if you will calm down, we can figure this out, but first I think you still have a bit of the problem left at your front door to clean up. I'll leave that to you. Besides, I've been trying to phone you for about two hours." He followed her back down the hall.

Francine was busy cleaning up the rest of the mess when the doorbell rang again. When she swung open the door, there stood a tall blond-haired man. By then, Francine's patience had dissolved.

"Who are you?" She screamed at him.

"I'm Mark."

"Mark? I told Debbie that I was not going to date you or anybody else . . ."

Before she could finish her sentence, Debbie came hurrying down the stairs, dressed in a pair of jeans and a pink blouse. "Hi Mark."

"Where are you going?" Francine asked.

"I'm going out with Mark. He's taking me for a ride on his bike. Mark, this is Francine."

The man shrugged his shoulders, held his hands into the air and signed quotation marks. "Why am I not surprised?"

The twosome walked out of the front door as Lillie and Marcie returned with the puppy. They could hear the roar of a motorcycle as Mark and Debbie rode away.

"We took her for a walk so she could use the bathroom." Lillie placed the puppy on the floor.

"You were a little bit too late." Francine replied, still holding the evidence wrapped in tissue paper in her hand.

"This is a cute little fellow. What are you going to name him?" It was Jackson this time inquiring as he reached for the pup.

"I've already told you. It's a she, and I'm not going to name her anything, because you are taking her away. Meagan sent this dog to thank me. I can't keep it. She couldn't have picked out a dog from her sick bed. Someone had to help her."

"Oh no. Looks like my little girl has struck again. I do remember her saying that she had a friend from school that had new pups. Sorry though, I knew nothing about this. Do you think she needs help in creating chaos? I'm on my way out of town again and need to be at the airport in about half an hour to be exact, and my plans don't include a dog or taking her anywhere. You'll have to keep her at least until I get back."

"Which is when?"

"Sunday evening."

"Sunday evening? If you didn't know about the dog, why were you trying to phone me?"

"I wanted you to look in on Meagan while I'm gone."

"As upset as I am, you'll trust me with your daughter. I was supposed to go to the beach for a quiet weekend." Francine called back over her shoulder as she walked toward the bathroom to get rid of the rest of the puppy's accident, taking short careful steps in case she'd missed something. The dog followed her every step, walking when she walked and stopping when she stopped. She returned, and the dog and everyone else followed her into the kitchen.

"She's really taken a liking to you." Lillie observed.

"C'mon, Lillie, let's you and me go upstairs and finish that project we started earlier."

"What project?"

Marcie grabbed her hand and pulled her toward the door. "You know, the project we were working on before we took the dog for a walk."

Lillie realized what she meant and hurried out with her.

"I'm really sorry, Francine. I'll take care of this when I get back. I simply don't have time now." Jackson shrugged, turning his palms upward.

"I thought you were finished with that merger. What are you going to do with her?"

"The dog or Meagan?" He tilted his head to one side with a serious look and crossed his arms.

They both laughed. "All right, I'll keep her until you get back?"

Jackson repeated, "The dog or Meagan?"

"So that's why you came over here to ask me to keep Meagan?"

"No, not keep her, but I would appreciate your looking in on her a couple times until I get back. She's still a bit peaked, and she really needs a friend. In addition, if you will do that for me, I'll see to a nice beach trip for you and your friends soon. You have my promise for a quiet weekend visit at my beach house to make up for all of this."

"All right. You have to promise to get this dog when you get back and have a talk with your daughter as well."

"What are you going to name her?" Jackson reached for the puppy that eagerly licked his face.

"I'm not going to name her anything. I am not going to keep her. Can anybody understand me? It is *not* my dog."

"She looks like a keeper. A fancy little thing. That's it. Why not call her Fancy?"

"Call her anything you like. I'll show you out before you miss your plane, and Fancy will be waiting for you when you get back." She had her hands propped on her hips, and she snapped her head forward to add emphasis.

Jackson carried the puppy to the front door, carefully placing her on the floor.

"Do you always sleep like that?" He pointed to what she was wearing.

Francine looked down at the worn flannel gown that reached almost to the floor. "Well, I'm covered. It's not usual for me to have company this late and unannounced."

"For your information, it's only eight-thirty in the evening. You are covered, but if you were my wife, you wouldn't be sleeping in that thing."

"Well, I'm not your wife. Besides, this is comfortable." Her voice was loud and Fancy sprang to her feet, ears perked. Jackson took a step toward her. Fancy let out several high pitched barks and bared her teeth.

He stepped back. "Fancy that. Looks like she's taken a liking to you. Guess you've stolen her and my little girl's hearts." He was still close enough to touch her nose with his finger.

She didn't answer, and Jackson turned to leave. "Oh, don't forget about the beach trip. I'm serious about making all of this up to you. We can plan that when I get back. There was another thing; I wanted to ask if you would . . ."

Before he finished, Francine waved her hand and said, "What the heck, whatever, I'll do it. I'll do it. Just tell me what Meagan needs. I seem to have lost control of my life."

"You will? Great. Next Friday evening. It's black tie."

"Black tie? Well, I'll be wearing my jeans to baby-sit your daughter and maybe some kind of armor would be in order. I guess the formal wear is for some highfaluting thing you're going to."

"You won't be baby-sitting my daughter next week. Mrs. Brown has already promised to stay with her. You'll be baby-sitting me in a way. That highfaluting thing we're going to is a banquet to celebrate the merger, and I'd like you to accompany me. See you Sunday night when I get back. Don't disappoint me."

"Why would I promise to look in on her and not go over there?"

"I was talking about the banquet."

Jackson's words sunk in, but before she could protest, he had hurried down the steps to his car, turning only long enough to give her that annoying salute.

She watched as he drove away. Fancy pulled at the hem of her gown. "All right, little fella. Guess you 're my guest at least for the weekend. Fancy my foot!"

"It's not a little fella, it's a she." Lillie and Marcie were back downstairs standing behind her.

Francine wondered how much they'd heard. "So, you two have been eavesdropping."

"Know what I think?" Marcie asked.

"No, Marcie, and I don't care what you think. But you are going to tell me anyhow, aren't you?"

"I think you have not only stolen that dog and that little girl's hearts, but Jackson Tanner's heart as well."

"I doubt it. He just wants a baby-sitter, and he has no interest in women."

"Then why is he taking you to a banquet and to the beach for the weekend?"

"He's sending all of us to the beach, and he has no one else to take to the banquet. Can't you understand that? It's my guess that the beach trip will involve another baby-sitting job for me. Anyone want to take bets on whether his little girl goes or not?"

"He's taking all of us? Great! Sure, we understand the rest. Jackson Tanner, the most eligible, handsome, rich man in town, who has no interest in women, doesn't have anyone but poor little Francine Bruckner to take to the ball. And, we'll help you *baby-sit* both of them at the beach." Marcie curled her lips and made them tremble.

Francine whirled toward the stairs, shaking her head in exasperation. She hadn't contemplated the fact that Jackson would be accompanying them to the beach. Fancy clamped her teeth tight onto Francine's gown as she went upstairs.

She made a little bed in the corner of the room for the puppy, turned out the light and once again stretched out. She felt the tiniest tug at the comforter with a scratching sound. After several attempts to get Fancy to sleep in the bed she'd made, Francine gave up the struggle and placed the puppy on her bed beside her. Fancy crawled up close, snuggled against the back of Francine's head, and went fast asleep.

She lay awake going over the events of the day. Francine slipped into a deep sleep and dreamed that she was riding in a carriage drawn by six Chihuahuas. She peered out the window to see Meagan dressed like Cinderella's fairy godmother. Only this godmother had horns, and instead of a wand, she held a tiny pitchfork. In the dream, she floated in the air with layers of chiffon billowing from her waist. The carriage delivered her to a large castle. When the door opened, Jackson Tanner stood there to greet her. However, as she reached for his hand, he backed away and faded into the foggy background.

Francine had made the statement many times that she never had dreams, but events of the past couple of weeks had changed all of that. She had dreamed of Jackson Tanner when her eyes were closed in sleep and in her mind when she was wide-awake. Neither sleep dreams nor those wide-awake ones proved to be satisfactory. She didn't want to fall in love with this man or any man, but she couldn't chase away the feelings. Her mind and heart were in constant conflict. Her mind reminded her heart that this kind of situation had proven to be unfruitful before. As the song goes, she'd "been cheated, been mistreated," but refused to ask the question, "when will I be loved?"

That night, she tossed and turned, waking every few minutes trying to re-arrange the puppy's position, but Fancy always snuggled back to the same spot as before, against her neck. When the two of them slept, the dream repeated itself throughout the night. It was the same scenario each time, with the Chihuahua drawn carriage delivering her across a puffy clouded sky to a beautiful castle. The door would open, and Jackson would be standing there with his hand extended. Their hands never touched, and a curious questioning look would always replace his smile as the figure backed away and faded into a heavy mist.

Chapter 5

ancy's wet kiss to her neck brought her out of her dream. After yawning and stretching, she succumbed to the puppy's persistence and said, "Come on girl, I'll take you out."

In the backyard, Francine made herself comfortable on the brick steps while Fancy ran about. Still sleepy, with elbows propped on her knees, she wished the pup would finish her business. The energetic little thing wanted to play and chased a couple of squirrels, who were nearly as big as she was. There'd never be a need for her to set the alarm as long as Fancy resided in the house. If only she could teach her about Saturdays being a sleep-in day.

Leaning back against the step, she stared at the top of the tall magnolia trees, drinking in their majestic beauty. She'd always loved the house, finding the backyard a place of comfort and solace even as a small child. When visiting her grandmother, Francine would play for hours alone here, going inside only at mealtime and near bedtime. Once having her bath, Grandmother Mailey would read Bible stories until either she or Francine became too sleepy. Closing her eyes, she could visualize the woman, small and delicate, standing in front of the kitchen sink. The sheer curtains floated in the soft breezes from the open window. She'd duplicated the decor with her own lace curtains and the fragrance of Ivory soap that drifted through the room.

"Here." It was Debbie, handing her a cup of strong, black coffee. All three of her housemates were special each in her own way, but Debbie was her best friend. It was Debbie who advised the others. It was Francine who was always there for Debbie.

"Thanks. You wouldn't believe the dream I had last night." They chatted as Fancy entertained herself looking for the squirrels who were well hidden by now. She related the dream to Debbie, and the two had a good laugh.

"There must be some hidden meaning in there somewhere. But, I wouldn't even dare try to analyze that one." Debbie poked her with an elbow.

"By the way, what's this with you and Mark?" Francine asked her.

"Well, you didn't want him. And, he's looking mighty good to me."

"He looks perfect for you. Don't know why you tried to put him onto me in the first place."

"My best friend was depressed and needed the best. You should've been more appreciative. However, I'm glad you didn't take him." Debbie drawled out the words and rolled her eyes.

"Sounds serious. Could it be? I've never seen you respond to anyone like you have to Mark. He's tall, blond-haired and successful -- what you've always wished. It's in your face." Francine rolled her own eyes in exaggeration.

"I hope it develops into something. He is easy to be with."

"There has to be more to it than that, Debbie. You're picky about your men."

"You are right about that. Not only is he comfortable to be with, he's considerate. Our backgrounds are similar. His parents died when he was quite young, and Mark is an only child. An aunt and uncle raised him. I lost both of my parents when I was a teenager, and I lived with my grandmother and grandfather until college. They were good to me, still are, yet they were older when I went to live with them and unable to be as involved in my doings as my parents would've been. They taught me a lot though. I'm glad they don't live so far away now. They're enjoying the small apartment in the housing complex with friends their own age. I can visit them anytime, and they can visit with me, thanks to you and your guest room." Debbie squeezed her arm and looked straight into her eyes and continued speaking, changing the subject back to Mark. "I think I may be falling in love with him."

"You think you may be? Strange how things work out. Debbie, you're such a great friend to me, always calm in any storm."

"You sound like *my* grandmother. Well, strange as this situation is, I hope things will work out for both of us." She gave Francine's arm another quick squeeze as Fancy came running back. "So, what are your plans for today?" Debbie asked.

Recalling her promise to Jackson, she said, "Guess I'll go over and check on Meagan. By the way, keep in mind the beach trip. It'll be fun for us to get away. I wonder what the place is like."

"Why is he letting all of us go?"

"He knows how close we are, and it wouldn't be much fun for me to go alone. I have a feeling that it will involve Meagan even though he indicated it's to make up for spoiling my plans and to show appreciation for taking her to the hospital and staying that night."

She left Debbie watching Fancy, and after breakfast, dressed and was soon out of the door and headed to the Tanner house. Meagan was chipper enough but still a bit weak. Mrs. Brown, the housekeeper, instructed her to have a nice visit while she went about her chores.

"Will you stay for lunch?" Meagan pleaded with her sweet voice and soulful eyes.

"I can't impose on Mrs. Brown. She has enough to do without having to make lunch for me."

"It's all right with Mrs. Brown. I already told her you'd be staying."

"Meagan, Honey. I need to talk to you about doing things like that. You shouldn't manipulate people into doing what you want. Perhaps Mrs. Brown should have the final say in the matter."

"She doesn't have any other plans. Here she comes now, I'll ask her."

"Ask me what?" Mrs. Brown brought in a large tray of sandwiches, milk and cookies, evidencing the fact that she expected Francine to stay for lunch.

"Didn't you say that you didn't have any other plans and you don't care if Francine stays for lunch?"

"No, my plans are to take good care of this young lady and this household, and upon special request from Mr. Tanner, I'm to make you comfortable while you're visiting our little angel here. And, don't worry, when she gets too bossy for me, I put her right back in her place." While she spoke to Francine, the woman brushed Meagan's hair away from her face and smiled at her.

"Thank you. I'm not so sure the title of little angel always fits." Francine gave a smile and a wink.

"She manipulates people, I'll agree, but it's in a good way most of the time. Besides, she'll always be my little angel." Mrs. Brown told her.

"I think there are horns holding up that halo." Francine reached over and gave Meagan a tug on her foot. "What about the nurse? The doctor had given Jackson the name of a nurse."

"Mr. Tanner agreed with me that I can take care of Meagan just fine, and if she needs a doctor, well, I have the phone numbers."

"Oh, I didn't mean anything. I just wondered."

"Shush now, I've been with them a long time. She will be fine now that you're here. I understand you are her pretend Mother."

"Sure she will." Francine nodded and despite herself, smiled at Mrs. Brown's last remark.

"What about your thank-you gift? Did you like it?" Meagan asked.

"Now, about that dog. She would be a perfect little companion for you."

"Thanks anyway, but I have Taffy, and they wouldn't get along."

"Taffy?"

"Taffy's her cat." Mrs. Brown said as she started out of the door. "Taffy's been here about as long as I have."

"I can't imagine what possessed this child to send a dog to me."

Mrs. Brown added, "No one knows what possesses this child." She added to Meagan, "After lunch, it will be time for a nap."

The two ate and chatted for about twenty minutes, and when Meagan began to yawn, Francine took it as her cue to leave.

Francine promised that she would visit again the next afternoon, which was Sunday but assured Meagan that she could give her a call anytime. She took the tray to the kitchen and tidied up before leaving.

After she returned home, Debbie asked if she'd said anything to Meagan about the puppy.

"Yes, not that it did any good. Between Meagan and Mrs. Brown, my arguments were lost to the wind. Mr. Tanner can take care of that little matter himself." Fancy was at her feet whining to be held. Francine picked her up, and she snuggled close.

The next afternoon Francine followed through on her promise and went back to the Tanner residence, taking Fancy with her. She made a mental note to keep the puppy away from Taffy. They played checkers for a while then Francine read several stories to Meagan. Taffy lay curled up beside Fancy on one side of Meagan. So much for the argument that the cat wouldn't like the dog or vice-versa.

When it was time for Meagan's nap, she pleaded with her not to leave. Francine switched off the light and said, "I'll stay here for a while." Francine crawled onto the bed beside the child, and the four of them were soon sound asleep.

When she awoke, it was dark in the room, and she lay there trying to get her eyes adjusted to the dark and realized someone had placed a quilt over her. Pushing the cover away, she tried to ease from the bed so as not to wake Meagan. A deep voice startled her.

"Are you awake?" A dark shadow came toward her.

Francine screamed and started swinging her arms, "Stay away."

The form grabbed and held her as she wiggled, still screaming. It was Jackson, and the only way to calm her was to put his hand over her lips. Taffy sprang from the bed and Fancy began barking.

By then, Meagan was awake, "Daddy, Daddy. You're home."

Francine became fully awake and aware of who was holding her. "I'm sorry. You can let me go now. I must have forgotten where I was for a moment."

He released her and she stepped backwards, hitting the tray on the night stand behind her, sending an unfinished glass of milk through the air to spatter all over herself, Jackson and the floor. Mrs. Brown came hurrying into the room and flipped on the light.

"My goodness, Mr. Tanner, did you forget where the light switch is?"

Francine grabbed a napkin and began mopping the floor.

Jackson stooped beside her and grabbed her hand. "Wait a minute. That glass is broken. You'll cut yourself."

It was too late and a stream of blood squirted from her hand. That too landed on Jackson's suit. Fancy jumped to the floor, growling and trying to tug at his pants leg. He stepped backward and onto the dog's foot. Fancy gave a yelp and ran from the room. Francine pulled her hand away and covered her mouth, shaking her head. "I'm so sorry, look at you. I've messed you up."

"In more ways than one. Hold your hand still. You're getting blood everywhere."

Jackson insisted on cleaning and bandaging her wound. She was so embarrassed that afterwards, she rushed from the house. When she realized she had left her purse and keys on the vanity in Meagan's bathroom, she hurried back inside. When she opened the bathroom door, it slammed into the back of Jackson; he'd removed all of his clothing except his boxers.

"What are you doing here?" She shrieked.

"I live here. This is the closest and most convenient place to remove my clothes to keep from dripping milk and blood down the hallway."

Francine backed out with her eyes clenched shut and right into Mrs. Brown who'd entered the room with a pan of soapy water to clean the carpet. The water sloshed over the woman who stood with her mouth gaping open.

"I'm so sorry. Now, look what I've done."

Meagan was giggling. "Oh, this is so funny."

"This is not funny." Francine's tears poured down her cheeks, and she dashed from the room and ran outside.

Once again, in her van, she realized that she still didn't have her purse or her keys or the dog. "Oh H-E-double toothpicks. I'll walk, and that darned dog is right where she belongs." She slammed the door to her van and started the hike homeward.

She had walked about a block when Jackson pulled alongside of her in his jag. "Would you like a little help from a friend? Get in the car." He drove back to his house and handed her the purse. "Is this what you were looking for?"

"You must think I'm the most stupid person in the world. I don't know why these things keep happening to me." She was still crying as she dug into the purse looking for her keys.

"Take my handkerchief. Now, that's better. We have to talk."

"Don't worry; I'll pay for the damages."

"Forget the damage. There was none. Nothing happened that a little soap and water can't take care of. I left a wet Mrs. Brown and a laughing little girl. So, not to worry. That's not what I wanted to talk to you about."

"Now, what? If it's about that dog."

"It's not about the dog. I wanted to let you know what the plans are for next Friday's banquet. I'll pick you up at six-thirty P.M., if that's not too early, so that we can arrive in time to check on the seating arrangements."

"Are you sure you want to take me? I may cause the building to burn down."

He laughed aloud. "Yes, I do want to take you, and I'm curious as to what else may happen. However, it's sure to be great entertainment. I may get the decorators to leave off the table candles."

"That's not funny, and it doesn't make me feel any better." She turned the key in the van then remembered to ask, "What are you going to do about your little problem?"

"Meagan?"

"Not that problem, the dog."

"This dog?" He reached inside his sweater, pulled the tiny pup out and plopped her into Francine's lap.

"No you don't."

While she was protesting, he turned, jumped back into his car and drove away from the house. Once she pulled the van onto the street, she felt the flip-flopping of a flat tire. "What more could happen?" Regardless, she would not go back into that house or give anyone there the satisfaction of knowing that she had yet another problem. She would drive home very slowly and call a garage from her own house. After going about three blocks, a flashing blue light appeared in her rearview mirror accompanied by a loud siren.

It was a young police officer strode up to the window; she rolled it down and faced him.

Before she could say a word, he asked, "Aren't you aware that you have a flat tire?"

"Yes, officer, but I'm going home, and I'll call a garage from there."

"Can't let you do that."

"Why not? It's not very far. I didn't want to stop in the dark, alone."

"Because riding on rims will ruin the pavement. Otherwise, no one would have to buy tires, thinking it would seem to save a bunch of money. However, riding on rims will ruin the highways, and that won't save taxpayers' money. Now, will it, Lady?"

Before she could even think of a reply, the silver jag appeared again and pulled to a stop in front of the van. Jackson stepped out shaking his head, motioning the officer to one side. They chatted as if they were long lost buddies. The officer returned long enough to tell her that he had called a wrecker at Jackson's instructions.

Francine refused to speak or look at Jackson who stayed until the wrecker came. She sat in the van holding Fancy while the work was being completed.

Jackson tapped on the window. "Everything's been taken care of. Are you and Fancy all right?"

"Wait just a cotton pickin' minute. Here you go, take the dog. This is not my dog."

He laughed and waved goodbye, leaving her sitting there with Fancy, who proceeded to cover her face with wet kisses.

She pulled bills from her purse and held them out of the window toward the mechanic.

"No thank you, Ma'am, Mr. Tanner told me to put this on his bill. We do a lot of work for him, and he always straightens up with us later."

"He's not responsible for my debts. Take this money."

"Can't do that anyhow."

"And, why not?"

"I'm not authorized to take payment. That has to be done through the office."

"Drat. You can at least take my name and address and mail the bill to me."

"Look, Lady, I have another call. Take it up with your boyfriend."

She turned away from him frustrated and infuriated. He shrugged his shoulders, shook his head and walked away, mumbling something about women.

Francine fussed and fumed all week. Meagan had called

to say she was lonely and wanted to talk. Marcie had answered the telephone while Francine was in the shower and listened to Meagan relate the events of her previous visit.

Marcie did, however, think to ask Meagan what her daddy planned to do about the dog. When she told Francine about the conversation, Francine asked, "What did she say her dad would do about the dog?"

"Nothing. He said it'd be a shame to take the poor puppy away now that she'd become so attached to you, after you'd named her and all."

"I didn't name the dog. He did." She exclaimed. Without thinking, she reached down to lift Fancy onto her lap.

So it went the following week. Fancy continued to match every step Francine made around the house. The puppy slept with her, stared at her as she dressed, and stayed on the bench in front of Francine's window every day while she was at work. As soon as Francine returned, Fancy would come bounding down the stairs, prancing about until she was taken outside. Francine always grumbled, "This is not my dog."

On one particular evening, Debbie had come through the house, dressed in leather pants, long sleeved shirt, carrying a heavy jacket.

"What's up, girlfriend? You really look sexy in that outfit."

Debbie responded, "Mark is coming to take me for a ride on his motorcycle. He told me to dress warm. Now, a word of advice to you. You have to quit grumbling about Fancy, and decide what you want to wear when you baby sit your man."

"He's not my man. I'm only going because . . ."

"Because you want to. Besides, you have to look sexy for that. Sounds like it may be quite an affair."

"Poor choice of words, Debbie. Could you say banquet?"

"O. K. Sounds like the banquet will be quite an affair." Debbie ducked just in time to miss the pillow from the sofa that Francine sent sailing through the air.

"You want to sit out front with me while I wait for Mark?"

"All right. If I don't hurry and take Fancy out, she'll explode."

Fancy ran about the front yard, marking her territory. This was the first time she ran free in front of the house. The girls became absorbed in conversation until they heard the sound of Mark's motorcycle. They screamed for Fancy at the same time and ran toward her. The puppy looked surprised and became confused, and thought they were angry with her. She ran the other way as Mark turned into the driveway. It was too late when he saw the puppy. He swerved and braked to avoid hitting her, but the bike skidded to a sideways fall. Fancy yelped and blood spurted from the tiny pup.

Mark began barking orders. "Debbie, call Dr. Best's office, and tell him we're on our way." He pressed on the spot to stop the flow of blood.

As Debbie ran inside, Mark pushed Francine away with his elbow, telling her, "Get into the van Francine, and drive as fast as you can. I'll carry Fancy and try and keep the blood stopped."

Marcie and Lillie pulled into the driveway stopping short of the motorcycle, and Mark called over his shoulder. "Bring Debbie. She'll explain."

Tears poured down Francine's face, and her eyes blurred as she drove. "Is she going to be all right?"

"I hope so. I'm so sorry. You've got to stop crying so you can see to drive, and hurry."

Francine turned on her emergency lights and drove quickly toward the vet's office as Mark gave directions.

"Mark. I know you didn't do that on purpose. This was my fault. I should never have let her run free in front of the house."

It took only minutes to reach Dr. Best's office. He was standing out front waiting and motioned for Mark to follow him. Francine could only wonder how the other three girls got there so fast. Before she could ponder that thought, in rushed Jackson and Meagan. Debbie had thought to call them.

Meagan rushed to Francine, nearly knocking her over when she hugged her. "Is she going to be all right? What happened?"

"It was an accident, Honey." She tried a reassuring smile as Mark came from the back, his clothes bloodstained.

As Debbie was explaining to Jackson, the front door opened again and a petite, sandy-haired woman walked in, followed by a beautiful golden retriever. She didn't stop or even slow up and headed toward the back.

"Now, where does she think she's going?" Francine started to follow her. "Would somebody tell her the doctor has an emergency here?"

Mark touched her on the arm and told her, "Don't worry, Francine, that lady is Shirley Best, the doctor's wife. That's Katie with her -- here to give Fancy blood if she needs it."

"Blood, you don't give a dog blood. If they lose too much blood, they just die."

Meagan gasped, and Francine was immediately sorry for her thoughtless words.

A vet tech came from the back. "Just wanted to reassure you. Fancy has lost blood, a lot for a little thing like her, and it's too soon to tell, but Dr. Best called his wife to bring Katie, just in case."

"That dog is really going to give blood? I've never heard of such." A white-faced Lillie, who'd not spoken until that moment, was led to a chair and ordered not to move.

The technician looked at Marcie and told her to follow him so he could get wet towels, in case Lillie needed them.

Before he left the room, he patted Lillie on the arm. "Katie is wonderful. Just what the puppy needs. We'll let you know something soon. I promise."

The sad group paced the floor for what seemed like hours until Dr. Best emerged. "She's not out of the woods yet, but Katie came through, as always. I can't promise anything. She'll have to stay here a few days, of course, but I think she'll pull through."

It was then that Shirley came into the waiting room and stood by her husband. "Bet you can't believe my Katie gives blood, huh? She's a regular trooper, knows exactly what's expected of her. We lower the table, and she walks right on to it and lies beside the patient. She knows she's helping."

"What about the blood? Human blood has to match. Doesn't hers?" Marcie asked.

"Thankfully, there have been many advances in veterinarian medicine, but I'll leave Shirley to explain. I need to get back to my patient." The doctor turned away.

Shirley picked up the conversation. "There are blood banks, but often they aren't close enough to do any good. Katie is a universal blood donor. Her blood can be used on any dog breed, and the best part for us is that she's close at hand and willing."

"You mean you don't have to worry about blood types?" Francine asked.

"Actually, dogs can be positive or negative. They have up to nine parts to their blood type, and because they can be positive or negative, there are thousands of different alternatives. A dog, like Katie, can be what is called a "universal" blood donor if he or she tests negative for all of the parts of blood types except the one called "DEA 4." Those are uncommon, so we're fortunate to have Katie. You can see she's precious, in more ways than just being my pet."

"That's the most amazing thing I've ever heard of." The entire group shared Lillie's awe.

Shirley continued, "Sometimes Sam will use her leg. She holds it right out for him, then remains still so he can do his job."

Meagan had remained silent, though her facial expression indicated her interest. "How did you find out she could do that?"

"We heard about the program and sent a sample of Katie's blood off to be tested and discovered she could be a universal donor. It worried me at first, but it works, and Katie doesn't seem to mind. Her blood is quick to build up, so there's no danger. So far, the demand hasn't been too much for her."

"I'm thinking I might like to work with animals when I grow up, especially with ones like Katie." Meagan was so serious that everyone laughed, and for the moment was relieved from Fancy's scare.

"I know you want to see Fancy, so I'll ask Sam if you can take a peek. You can go on the internet and find out more about animal donors, if you're really interested."

Each one of them was allowed to peek in on the sedated Fancy. The tech had volunteered to stay with her all night, but everyone else would have to go. He had lots of experience and knew what to do in case of an emergency. However, he was quick to accept Lillie's offer to go home, prepare a thermos of coffee and return, in case he needed someone with him. Amused looks passed between the others when they realized that Lillie wanted to be near him as much as she wanted to be there for Fancy. They left with a promise to reward Katie later with her favorite food -- saltine crackers.

A few days later, they held a joint welcome home party for Fancy and thank-you for Katie. Though still weak, Fancy showed her delight as she curled up on a special new doggie bed and raised her head to give wet kisses to everyone there. She even ate some of Katie's saltines.

Francine had found it difficult to sleep without the puppy being snuggled close to her neck, but that evening, they both were fast asleep by nine P.M. Francine was too exhausted to dream.

Chapter 6

The other three girls busied themselves with pressing her dress, helping with the final touches of makeup, or holding mirrors so that Francine could check herself from every angle. Before Jackson arrived, the four knew they'd achieved perfection in the way Francine looked. They decided on a long, black, clingy dress with spaghetti straps and a slit on one side. The shoes, black satin, had tiny pearls on each strap and matched her evening bag.

The content of her purse was the only thing that Francine had any say about. It contained lipstick, facial tissues, a small pocketknife, a mirror, comb, and a change purse with a few bills and coins. She smiled, remembering her mother's advice, "always, take mad money."

"Mad money?" She'd asked.

Her mother's response had been with a twinkle in her eye. "It all depends on the distance you're going." As she became older, she realized it didn't have all that much to do with miles.

"Why are you putting all that stuff in there? You know you won't need it. Why don't you let him carry your lipstick? Why do you have a pocketknife?" The questions came, one after the other, without waiting for Francine to answer.

"That's right, Francine. You don't need all of that." Marcie added.

"I always carry a pocketknife, comes in handy. Married women stick their lipstick in their husbands' pockets. You don't do that with a date. Besides, you never know when you might need a pocketknife. Did you know, men don't carry them anymore? Not men who work in offices and dress in fine suits. My daddy was a hard-working electrician. He always carried a pocketknife."

"Well, when have you needed one?" Marcie asked, beginning to sound like curious Lillie.

"As a matter of fact, a couple of days ago. A woman had purchased one of those small plastic swimming pools. The person at the store tied it on top of her car with a heavy string. The wind blew it off. I stopped to help, and so did a man in a suit. He had no pocketknife and seemed amazed that I should ask him for one. I not only had heavy cord in my van, but there was my handy knife. Fixed her right up; followed her home to make sure it stayed secure."

"And, embarrassed the man." Marcie grinned.

"I hope it embarrassed him. When the woman thanked me, she said she was going back to the store the next day for heavy cord and a pocketknife. I also told her to fix herself up a little box with other emergency items that she may need in the future."

"Well, remember that you can't take that thing on an airplane." Lillie furnished the information as if they had never heard that before.

"I know that. Besides, I don't plan to fly anywhere soon. I promise to leave my knife and heavy cord home, in your care, if I do."

All of the girls became a bit nervous, and Debbie's eyes teared up. "Wait!" She rushed from the room, coming back with her new black shawl that sparkled with tiny sequins.

"No, I don't need that."

"Yes, you do. Take it off when you think that it will have the best effect on Jackson when he sees your dress and that bit of cleavage."

"Quit. You'll make me blush."

"You should. It's quite becoming." Marcie remarked.

Francine patted her hair once more, pleased with her story and the way she looked.

"This is it, girls -- I hear a car."

"You stay right here, and we'll let him in." Debbie motioned to the other girls.

"Please, don't all of you go. Marcie, you and Lillie, stay here with me."

"No. We want to watch you come down the stairs *and* to see Jackson's face when he sees you."

They were standing in their appropriate places, but they hadn't foreseen that she would stumble. With a quick prayer, she was able to grab the banister in time, but wondered if Jackson's gasp was his response to her appearance or the fact that he thought she'd fall. He walked to the bottom of the staircase and held out his hand. As soon as they touched, Fancy rushed over, grabbed his pants leg, tugged at it with her teeth and growled. The tension was broken and everyone laughed.

"My, she's getting to be a possessive little thing."

As soon as they reached the banquet hall, someone named Joan, wearing a long, red dress, complete with sequins that sparkled like tiny diamonds, whisked Jackson away. Francine was sure that the dimmed lights created the effect Joan desired. She watched Joan holding onto Jackson's arm and escorting him around the entire room. They stopped at each table to examine the centerpieces. At the head table, Joan pointed to the seats as she spoke. Jackson didn't appear pleased. They walked toward the kitchen, and Francine assumed that was to review the menu with the chef. Joan returned to Francine and motioned toward a table in a dark corner. She informed Francine that would be her place.

Jackson had walked over to greet his parents. Francine shrugged, leaving the wicked witch of all directions. She walked around the room enjoying the picturesque scene of the massive fireplace located at one end and the beautiful pictures of huge oak, magnolia trees, and antebellum mansions, including one of

Wisteria Inn where the banquet was being held. The room was infused with a true southern atmosphere, giving her soul peace as memories of Grandmother Mailey and the tall magnolia trees in her own backyard, wove through her mind. She didn't hear Jackson or Joan as they walked up behind her.

Joan spoke with a condescending tone giving just enough cordiality to her phony graciousness. "Sorry to leave you alone, Dear, but there's so many details to be confirmed. Come, and I'll take you to your table. I do believe you might be more comfortable if you go ahead and find your place."

"Thanks, I believe I'll be able to find it myself." She tossed her head, refusing to look at Jackson. Even Francine knew that it was inappropriate for the host's date to sit alone. At any rate, no one would notice her tucked away by herself nor see her if she made some stupid mistake, like tripping the waiter, or setting the building on fire.

"Where will Jackson be sitting?" She asked in an innocent tone, speaking to Joan but looking toward Jackson who stood with a wrinkled brow. She placed two fingers to her forehead in mock salute as he turned to walk away. Looking back, his frown turned to a grin when she stepped on the hem of the wicked witch's dress. There was the sound of an ever-so-slight tear.

"I'm sorry." Francine asked, "Did I step on your gown?"

"Not to worry, Dahling. You can't hurt this old thing. Jackson will sit to the right of the podium, and I will sit next to him. See, he's over there checking his place now. He has to make a speech, but there's only so much room at the head table, what with the officers and all. I'm sure you won't mind watching from here." The last sentence had an indication of question mark at the end.

"No, of course not." She agreed because she had no choice. Francine excused herself and found the ladies' room and entered one of the stalls. While she was adjusting her stockings, the voices of others rang loud and clear.

It was Joan and another woman. Francine decided to do the

opposite of what her sweet grandmother had always warned her. "Don't eavesdrop, Dear. If you do, expect to hear what you don't want to hear."

That's what happened.

"No, I stuck her off by herself in the dark. I don't know what his idea was in inviting her. I paid $900.00 for this dress to dazzle Jackson, and she won't get near him if it's left up to me. She must be some kind of clumsy idiot, the way she spills everything, from what I hear. Good grief, she even stepped on my hem. I thought I heard a tear."

Francine waited until the women left the room. Too angry to cry, she hurried to her seat, slamming her purse down so hard, its contents spilled onto the table with some falling to the floor. As she was scrambling to gather it up, she noticed Jackson watching her from across the room, and this time his look was very serious, so she assumed her clumsiness had managed to embarrass him. "Oh well, what the hay." By now, Francine could not have cared less. If only the next few hours would speed by, she would be home away from all this silliness. Seated near the kitchen, she knew there was a back door for a quick getaway, if necessary.

Before walking to the podium, Jackson turned to one of the waiters and whispered. She noticed that his mother and father and two other couples were seated to his left. Two couples sat to Jackson's right, and according to protocol, Jackson and his date should sit between them and the podium. However, Joan stood behind one of the empty chairs, looking a bit startled when the waiter arrived to remove one of the place settings. While two waiters arranged another place at Francine's table, she heard the gentle tapping of Jackson's fork against a glass.

"I'm told that after dinner, I'm supposed to make a speech. However, the real honor for that will go to Dad," Jackson nodded toward his dad and continued, "and to Wilson over here to my far right. Both of them have worked hard on this merger and are much better at making speeches than I am, so I'll leave them to it." Hesitating a moment, he said, "It is, however, my privilege to welcome you tonight and to express my gratitude to each of you who have worked so hard to complete this deal. Make yourselves comfortable, and may you and your spouse or date have a lovely evening. Our minister, The Reverend Spruell, will give the invocation, but first I would like to acknowledge and introduce my date for this evening. She's the lovely lady who is holding my place over there. Francine, how about waving to our guests."

Stunned, she lifted her hand and waved as Jackson added, "Permission is granted for you to smile at them as well. She has a beautiful smile, don't you agree?"

Francine heard the crowd applaud and she did smile, but it was because of the look of sheer anger on Joan's face as she stared at the back of Jackson making his way to where Francine sat. Jackson was smiling also, and as he walked, he shoved his hands into his pockets. As soon as he reached his place at the table, he placed two fingers beside his temple adding a wink to his salute. She only worried what Rev. Spruell was thinking, or if he knew the story about Meagan's pretend mom.

After dinner and the very brief speeches from Wilson and Mr. Tanner, the band began playing, and Jackson pulled Francine to her feet and led her to the dance floor. She thought the maneuver was a bit abrupt and then realized why when she looked over at Joan who was in a half rise with a look of dismay. It was apparent that she had the idea to snatch Jackson away again. Francine snuggled close to him, eyes closed, as he pressed his face against her hair. With each turn, she managed to open at least one eye to enjoy the glare on Joan's face. Another perfect evening. Well, almost perfect. She only bumped into two waiters, causing them to spill drinks they were carrying on trays, and stumbled over the strap of one lady's handbag. Jackson caught her before she landed in the lap of the woman's husband. After each song, Jackson held her in place and Francine assumed it was to keep Joan away. At least, she hoped that was the reason. As if planned, several men kept Joan on the dance floor.

After this almost perfect evening, they arrived home. Outside her door, Jackson reached for Francine drawing her close. She'd puckered for the kiss when Marcie snatched open the door. They stepped apart.

"Sorry. Thought that might be you, but there's a call. It's Jerry."

"Jerry who?" Francine asked.

"Jerry, the guy you were engaged to."

Upon hearing those words, Jackson's mood changed, and he turned away. "See you later." He called over his shoulder.

"Did you have to open the door just then?"

"I said I'm sorry. The phone is for you, and that dog has cried all evening. Won't go outside, just hides when I go near her. I've had it."

She went inside and reached for the phone, "Yes, Jerry, what do you want?" She didn't intend to be polite. It was the first she had heard from him in weeks or was that months? She no longer counted because she no longer cared.

Jerry explained to her that he was getting married, and the wedding would be very soon. Hoping there were no hard feelings, he wished that she and her roommates would attend.

"Well, congratulations. Next Saturday, 3:00 P.M. Yes, I have it, and I'll try to be there."

She turned to tell Debbie the news that Jerry would be getting married the next Saturday and the four of them had been invited.

"Somehow, I don't think you mind." Debbie said.

"You are right. I don't mind." With that, she yawned and headed upstairs with Fancy in tow.

"Oh no, you don't. You won't get away without telling us in detail about this evening." Debbie told her.

"Maybe tomorrow."

"Tomorrow won't cut it. We've been involved in this date from the beginning. We've stayed up waiting to hear the details. You won't get away from us. Come on, coffee's ready. Let's have it."

She related the details of the evening, and they laughed until tears came down their cheeks. They laughed hardest at the part about the tear in Joan's dress and "that old thing" that only cost her $900.00.

Since Jackson didn't call, her mood spiraled downward, but she kept busy with preparations for an interview and pictures by the <u>County Magazine.</u> Her business would be featured in its next issue, and it would mean great advertising. The meeting was scheduled for Friday afternoon. After lunch on that day, Francine was headed back to her office, and when she entered the elevator, there was Jackson.

"Hi, Francine. How are you?"

"Fine. I want to say thank you again for a lovely evening at the banquet."

"And, I want to tell you congratulations." He commented.

Thinking he meant the feature in the magazine, she replied, "Thanks. How did you find out? We only agreed last week."

"Last week? News travels fast in this building. Will you still work?"

"Yes, and harder than ever, I hope."

"That would be a bit trying, don't you think?"

"It's what I've been hoping for."

"Of course. I thought perhaps you were getting over it."

"I've been dreaming of this for a long time."

"It just goes to show you that some dreams do come true."

"It's not that big a deal. The business is only going to be featured in the <u>County Magazine</u>. They aren't paying me. If it brings in the added business we're hoping for, it will be a dream come true. . . You aren't talking about the magazine feature, are you?"

"No. I'm talking about the marriage. Of course, most women

don't want to work after they are married. But you seem to be the exception to most rules."

"Married?" The elevator stopped, and Jackson got off and started walking away. "I'm not getting married." She managed to say as the door closed.

She started punching buttons, and the elevator stopped on the fifth floor. When it opened, she shouted, "I'm not getting married!"

The young couple standing there stepped backward and stared, the girl huddled close to the boy with a mixed look of fear and surprise, and the door closed again. Off she went, once again punching buttons until the elevator stopped on the eighth floor where Jackson had gotten off. He stood there waiting as the door opened and jumped into the elevator again.

"Did you say that you're not getting married?"

"No. Yes, that's what I said. I'm not getting married. Where did you hear such a thing?" The door once again opened on the fifth floor, and the young couple was still standing there. They stepped back, and Francine yelled at them, "Are you getting on or not?"

They backed away, and the young man said, "No thank you. We'll take the stairs."

The door closed, and Jackson spoke. "It's rumored about the building that you were getting married, and Jerry did call you the other night."

"He called to invite me to his wedding."

"That's just great." Jackson kissed her cheek, the door opened on the eighth floor, and Jackson hurried out. The door closed again.

When she emerged from the elevator on the second floor, she saw the young couple speaking to the security guard and pointing in her direction. They were quick to walk away as she approached them. A safe distance from her, they stood together glaring at

Francine and the guard. With a disgusted look, they turned to leave when they saw the security guard laughing.

After she explained what had happened, he realized they'd been talking about Francine and calling her the weird woman on the elevator. He asked, "Where's the man you had with you? And, what's all this talk about you getting married You're the talk over the entire building?"

Francine glanced in the direction of the young couple and said, "I ate him." Then she licked her fingers one by one. They turned and hurried the other way. "Nothing about marriage. It was all a misunderstanding. Just a rumor."

She was still smiling when she arrived at her office. Everyone had a good laugh when she told them about the incident. Her mood was uplifted in time for the interview. Lillie had brought Fancy in and announced that she was the company mascot and should be included in the photos. Fancy, feeling her importance, was on her best behavior and appeared to pose for the reporter.

It had been a long week, but Francine felt much better now that Jackson was aware she wasn't getting married. She hoped that was the reason he hadn't called. The thought did occur to her though, that he hadn't mentioned anything about the two of them getting together.

Oh well, she mused in the Scarlett O'Hara tone, "I can't think about that now. Tomorrow is soon enough, and 'after all, tomorrow is another day.'"

Chapter 7

The four girls packed and repacked their suitcases as if they were going for a two-week stay at the beach, not two days. They placed everything in the van so they'd be ready to leave right after work the next day. Each girl would work until lunchtime, meet back at the house and get Fancy. Then, they would pick Meagan up, and Jackson would join them early Saturday morning.

Lillie put their favorite CD in the player, turned the music up to its loudest volume, and they listened as it drifted upstairs. The four were so engrossed with enthusiastic conversation, that they never turned on the TV or radio to check the weather.

Fancy shared their excitement and pranced behind Francine's every step. She seemed hurt and a bit confused when everyone left Friday morning without her. She didn't understand that they would come for her before they left for the trip.

When they returned home that afternoon to pick up the dog, they found that she'd pulled a roll of toilet tissue from the hall bathroom, trailing it along the way. Annoyed at being left behind, she'd ignored the potty pads and left evidence of toilet needs in a couple of spots. The milk in her bowl had been overturned. It caused a thirty-minute delay to clean up the mess. From time to time, the sun slipped behind the clouds, and the wind had picked up a bit but not enough to appear threatening.

It was a three-hour drive to the beach, and Meagan sat up front with Francine and chatted all the way. Debbie had been out late with Mark the night before, so she slept. Lillie and Marcie played cow poker. Marcie explained the game to Meagan. Each person would count the cows they passed on their side of the road. If the pasture was full, they could only add ten cows to their total. If they passed a cemetery, this meant that all of the cows for that side had died, and the player's score dropped to zero.

"Who made up that game?" Meagan asked.

"I don't know. It's an old game. My brother and I played it when we were children and traveled with our parents." Francine told her.

"Why?"

"It makes the time pass by faster."

She giggled and remarked, "Francine, you can't make time pass by faster."

"It makes you feel like time is passing faster. Especially if you're really excited about where you're going."

"Are you excited?" Meagan kept a constant banter going.

"I suppose so."

"Suppose so? Aren't you really excited?"

"Yes, Meagan, I am really excited. I love the beach, although this was not the trip I had in mind."

"What did you have in mind?"

"My original plans were to spend a very quiet couple of days reading."

"We messed up your plans."

"No, you didn't mess them up. This is only a variation. Besides, nothing can be greater than being together with good friends."

"But, you are excited?"

"Yes, Meagan, I'm excited. I love the beach."

"Is that all, or are you excited that Daddy will be coming down tomorrow?"

"Why don't we play cow poker?"

"I don't want the time to pass by faster. I love riding in this neat van. I've been to the beach before."

"You like the beach, don't you, Meagan?"

"Yeah, but it's not as much fun anymore. My cousins are so involved with dance and piano and basketball, they don't have much time to come with us."

"Why don't you join in some of those activities?"

"I did start taking piano lessons, but after Mum died, I missed so many lessons, I didn't get started back."

"I think you should take it up again. How long did you play?"

"About a year."

"Think about it. You would love it. I play the piano."

Meagan's entire attitude changed. "That's great. Will you teach me, please, please?"

Francine laughed at the young girl's enthusiasm. "I can't teach you, but I do know the right person who can, and I could come to all of your recitals, if you promise to introduce me as your friend." She added that part with a sideways glance.

"Why can't you teach me?" Meagan's smile indicated she understood the implication.

"I'm not a piano teacher. You need an expert for that."

"Would you really come to all my recitals?" She clapped her hands and squealed so loud that she woke Debbie.

"What in the world's going on?" Debbie asked.

They filled her in on the details, and things settled down for the remainder of the trip. Every now and then, Meagan would think of a question that would entail a whole line of additional questions and answers. When they reached the beach area, Meagan gave directions to the house. It was secluded from the main road, and it had a long, paved driveway. There was an eight-foot cement privacy fence surrounding it, and the entire area had a beautiful landscape. There were shady, oak trees filled with Spanish moss. An Olympic size pool was on one side of the house and a huge veranda on the other side decorated with beautiful black wrought iron furniture. A screened-in porch with wicker furniture faced the ocean and ran all the way across the back of the house. The spacious yard had palm trees, a tree house for Meagan and a long, winding pathway that led to a private portion of the beach.

After Meagan showed them around the yard, they noticed that the wind seemed to be picking up. She pointed out the small dressing rooms for swimmers' use and then, led them from the porch to the mudroom outside the kitchen to continue the tour inside. As gorgeous as the yard was, it in no way prepared them for the inside of the house. Moving through the full-sized kitchen with its sparkling appliances, they walked into a large den, which held sofas, love seats, a television set, card tables and a pool table. French doors opened to a sidewalk that ended poolside.

"Wow!" exclaimed Lillie. "Did you say you had a beach house? Looks more like a hotel. Who keeps this place clean? We need a map."

"You're funny, Lillie." Having to keep the place clean had never concerned Meagan. She continued. "Come on, and I'll show you your rooms. Each of you can have your own bedroom, or you can share."

Francine noted that each of the bedrooms had two queen-sized beds, a bathtub and a shower. She said, "I don't think it will be necessary or practical for us to take separate rooms. Debbie and I can take a room together and Lillie and Marcie can take a room together."

"That means I have to stay in my room all by myself."

Lillie said, "I have a better idea. Debbie, Marcie and I can stay together and you and Meagan can stay in her room."

"Hot dog. That will be perfect. Will you, Francine?"

"Sure. That's fine by me. Where's your room?"

"Right across the hall from Daddy's room. Grandma and Gramps have their suite at the other end by the den. That was on the side where the porch stopped. They have a little private patio and a pavement that leads to the pool from their area."

Lillie rolled her eyes at the child before asking, "You can't mean there's more to this house?"

"Sure is, and there's a hallway from their suite which also leads to the outside of the house, and they can get to the main kitchen from there."

"Unbelievable." Debbie said, and the other girls shook their heads in agreement, not commenting on her remark about the *main* kitchen. "Come on, and I'll show you the food." Meagan grabbed Francine's hand.

"Shouldn't we go to the store, Meagan, and buy food and not use yours?" Francine asked.

"Nope, Daddy has a couple of folks who are responsible for cleaning and stocking up on everything so it's always ready when we get here. The lady's husband has a landscaping business, so he takes care of the yard. See the air-conditioning is already on. It may be a little cool in here. We can adjust it. Do you want to eat? Do you want to go for a late swim in the Ocean or pool? Do you want to bring in the suitcases?" That answered the question of who kept the place clean. It was obvious there had to be an army of yard workers.

"Yes to everything, except the swimming. Let's wait on that. It's a bit late, and I think the wind is picking up." Marcie laughed as they rushed from the house to gather their things.

Francine unpacked and stretched out on her bed while the other three retired to their chosen room to do the same. Later, she opted for a bubble bath and was surprised when Meagan took a short nap. Nearing suppertime, everyone emerged from their rooms about the same time.

Meagan insisted they cook steaks and potatoes. With no sensible reason to disagree, they headed to the kitchen where they found all the fixins' for salad with an array of dressings to choose from. As if that was not enough, they completed the meal by having vanilla bean cheesecake slathered with whipped topping.

Later, the five of them settled in their gowns. Meagan popped in a movie, and they all nibbled on popcorn -- the scene looked like an old-fashioned pajama party. Then . . . they heard the front door opening.

"Oh no, we need to cover up." Lillie grabbed a throw from the back of the sofa while Marcie and Debbie ran from the room.

Francine stood, or at least tried to, but the leg crossed beneath her had gone to sleep and gave way sending her sprawling across the floor in an undignified manner. The bowl of popcorn was tossed into the air, sending the white puffballs across the floor.

"Oh, Francine." Meagan told her, "It's Daddy."

Francine scrambled to pull her short nightshirt down as Jackson stroke across the room and held out his hand. Fancy, who'd not moved when everyone else scrambled, bared her teeth and growled.

"Can't you teach your dog manners?" He grinned as he spoke. "One day, she might hurt somebody. Then, you'll have trouble."

"That's not my dog, Jackson Tanner. Turn yourself around, and I'll get myself up, if you please." Even after Fancy's accident, she was reluctant to claim the dog, although her protests about ownership had become quite weak.

"I'm pleased." Jackson turned his face to the other direction. By then, Fancy had planted her teeth into Jackson's pants leg, pulling as hard as she could. She couldn't do real damage.

Without turning around, Jackson said, "This is an expensive suit, so if you don't mind, would you please get your Tasmanian devil away from me." He was smiling at the determination of the tiny dog.

"I repeat. She's not my dog." Francine called back as she scrambled to her feet and hurried from the room where she pulled on a pair of shorts and tee-shirt. By the time she returned, Jackson had a vacuum and was busy removing what Meagan had said, *Looked like snow.*

"I can finish getting that. We didn't know you were coming tonight."

"That's obvious." He flashed a smile, "I finished up early, so thought I'd come down and keep you girls company, since it is also obvious you haven't listened to the news. There's quite a bit of wind and rain on the way."

"Weathermen seldom have the forecasts correct so we don't rely on them." Debbie commented, waving her hand dismissing any idea of bad weather disturbing a perfect trip.

"Ladies, you don't need the weatherman to tell you it's windy, however, if he is correct, there's a pretty good storm brewing. If he doesn't have it right, there should be a terrific sunrise visible from the back porch tomorrow morning." Jackson kept vacuuming.

"Great, Daddy. Will you wake everyone up so we can watch it together?"

"Meagan, you say that every time, then you won't get up."

Lillie remained on the couch snuggled beneath the soft throw.

"What are we going to do?" Debbie inquired as she re-entered the room fully dressed.

"Get up early and watch the sunrise if we don't have a problem with the weather." Meagan told her.

Jackson turned toward Francine as he spoke. "It seems that the hurricane off the coast of Florida that was moving out to sea may decide to turn inward. If so, it'll bring some heavy wind and rains, but that won't happen until late tomorrow, if at all."

"Oh? I didn't know there was a hurricane on the way." Francine tilted her head.

"Like I said, you girls must never watch the news." Jackson finished with the vacuum and put it away.

"Not often. We do housework, cook, then play cards or something in the evening. We aren't much into television." Debbie explained.

"Most of the time, we listen to the music from our CD player." Lillie offered further explanation. "Tonight, all we've done is unpack, take long luxurious baths, naps and eat. By the way, have you eaten?"

Jackson shook his head in the affirmative.

"What's the name of the hurricane, Daddy?"

"Uh, I forgot."

"Think. What is it?" Meagan persisted.

Trying to hide his amusement, Jackson looked toward her as he said, "Francine."

"What?" Francine asked.

"Francine."

"I said what?"

"What nothing. That's the name of the hurricane." He and Meagan doubled over with laughter and were soon joined by the other three.

"Very funny." Francine stood, tossed her head backward and started to leave the room. Turning back, she noticed Fancy had likewise tossed her head backward and was following her.

"Daddy, that's great. Why did they name it after Francine?"

She tiptoed back to the end of the hallway to listen to his explanation.

"The weatherman said it was chaotic in a . . ." Jackson eased toward the edge of the room near where Francine was standing and continued, "nosy kind of way."

Meagan and the other girls laughed but with Jackson getting closer to Francine, Fancy became annoyed and ran toward him growling. Francine went into her room and slammed the door where she stayed until Debbie came in.

"Forget something?"

"Why don't you take that dog to its rightful owner?"

"This dog can't stand Jackson Tanner. She would eat him up."

"Do you realize how little that dog weighs? I doubt he could eat up one hundred seventy five pounds of . . ."

"Yes?" Debbie waited for an answer while still holding the dog.

"Whatever. Give me the darned dog." Fancy snuggled close to Francine and closed her eyes in sleep. Meagan came into the room for a chat, but she and Francine soon joined Fancy in sleep.

A knock on the door woke them early the next morning. It was Jackson. "It's time to see the sunrise."

"Oh no. I just went to sleep, and I don't want to see any sunrise." With that, Francine turned over and covered her head. Then, she remembered she shouldn't disappoint Meagan, but tried to no avail to rouse the child from her deep sleep.

Jackson spoke from the other side of the door, "Don't take time to primp. It won't wait forever."

"I'm coming." She called out, but mumbled to herself, "Does he really think I'd primp for him?" She pulled on jeans and a shirt, gave a quick brush through her hair and popped a breath mint into her mouth.

Jackson was waiting on the porch. "It's a lovely view, but I'm afraid Francine has done her dirty work. The sunrise is not what I had hoped for at all, too cloudy. Rain is on the way."

"Don't you think it's a bit chilly out here?"

"Hmmm. It's been a bit chilly for a while now."

"What is that supposed to mean?"

"Come here." He held up a small blanket for her to wrap in. When she turned, he held onto both sides. Wrapped in his arms, she leaned back, with no complaint.

"Better?"

"Yes. It is."

"Warmer?"

"What do you mean by that? Let go of me, now."

"I didn't mean anything." He was laughing as she jabbed her elbow into his side.

Her shuffling made him lose balance, and the two of them crashed to the floor. Fancy chose that moment to come bounding onto the porch, jumping into the middle of them. She bit Jackson on the nose.

"Get your dog away from me."

"That is not my dog. Are you hurt?"

"My nose is stinging. What do you think?"

"I think it serves you right. Nobody else bothered to get up to see a sunrise that isn't there. I'm going to take your dog for her morning walk."

"Don't be long. Breakfast will be ready in a little while. I'll cook after I get stitches in my nose." He called after her.

"You don't have to cook breakfast for me."

"Not for you, for everyone. Thirty minutes."

Fancy ran along the beach, but every few feet, she would stop and wait for Francine. It was cool, and Francine knew she should have worn a sweater. The blush from the memory of Jackson's arms around her only warmed her face. She would not go back before the thirty minutes were up. The heavy morning dew became light rain. The breeze grew stronger. Francine wrapped her arms about herself, shivering, and called for Fancy.

"Let's go back now, girl." Fancy ignored her.

A large Doberman loped toward them seemingly from nowhere. She knew he wasn't menacing, but his playful bark terrified Fancy. She tucked her tail between her legs and ran. Francine spurred into action, but the frightened puppy disappeared into the thick verdant growth farther down the beach. She followed Fancy's yelping until she could no longer hear her. Two hours later, with the wind whipping about her, thoroughly drenched, exhausted, cold and lost, Francine heard Jackson and Meagan calling her name. . .

"When you didn't come back, I thought you were angry, but we waited for another half hour, and then decided we'd better look. We've been searching for over an hour."

The rain came, full force. She tried to explain what had happened and started crying. "I can't find her."

"Now, don't worry, we'll find her. There's a patrol out now warning people to be prepared in the event of the need to evacuate. Shouldn't be dangerous here, but you never know the mind of a hurricane." There was a slight quirk to the corners of his lips, giving Francine the idea that he was remembering the name of this particular storm.

Jackson had brought along a warm, woolly sweater, and an extra raincoat. "Here, slip the raincoat on, then you may be able to slide out of your blouse and put the sweater on." He held an umbrella over her while she did as he instructed.

They saw one of the patrol cars and waved to the driver. He proved to be of no help because he was too busy trying to get people off the beach, suggesting that they prepare to leave the island if necessary.

"We'll keep an eye out for the dog and call you if we find her. Give me your cellphone number in case you decide to leave the island."

"Are you crazy? Do you think I'm going to pack up and leave without my dog?" Francine realized for the first time, she had claimed ownership.

"No, Officer. We have to find her." Jackson told the man. "We'll keep looking. Of course, we'll leave if we feel that it's necessary."

"All right, I'll let you stay out here for a little while, but you'll have to leave if it becomes hazardous." After writing the number on his pad, the man drove off.

Meagan tugged at her arm, "So, you love the dog now?"

"Of course, I love the dog."

"You're going to keep her forever and forever?"

"Forever and forever may be debatable, Meagan – if we find her."

"You called her your dog."

"I know. Sometimes it takes losing something before you realize how much you care."

"Let's at least get you back and warmed up. Then we'll look for *your* dog some more." Jackson led the way.

They saw the other girls coming toward them. They all ran back to the house. Francine discovered she'd lost her bearing and had been a few blocks away. When they returned, they found a safe and dry Fancy, sound asleep curled up beneath the canopy on one of the chairs.

Francine, the storm, brought strong winds and rain, before turning away from land, so they decided to stay until Sunday, after all. They were safe, and it would be foolish to try to drive back in the weather. The remainder of the time was spent playing cards, eating, and enjoying the relaxation. Francine also managed to get in a few hours of reading. All too soon, it was time to pack up and leave. Jackson promised them another trip the first pretty weekend.

Meagan had been noticeably quiet during the remainder of the stay, and Francine feared she may have caught something, but the child had no temperature. Meagan rode with Francine while the other girls rode with Jackson.

When they reached the Tanner home, Francine emphasized to Jackson that he should keep a watch on Meagan in case she was getting sick. He promised to have Mrs. Brown on guard as well. "Yes Ma'am." He saluted as the other girls exited his vehicle to ride home with Francine.

"I do believe I'd better get a warm bath, take some cold medicine myself, just in case, and head for the bed," Francine announced. "I feel a bit warm."

The other three girls snickered but remained quiet as they headed home. The medicine proved to be a good idea, and it helped her sleep. After being drenched while searching for Fancy, she did end up with a severe cold. By early morning, her temperature rose to one hundred two degrees, and she phoned her doctor. He prescribed strong medicine and ordered her to bed for the next few days. Faced with inactivity and boring daytime TV, she welcomed the sleep the medicine provided. On the second day, she and Fancy moved downstairs to the couch.

One evening, Jackson came by with homemade chicken soup prepared by Mrs. Brown. He brought enough for all of the girls to have a couple of meals. Mrs. Brown included a pan of delicious cornbread. Her message was, "If you other girls aren't sick, this will keep you well."

"I'll be right back." He left the house and returned with sweet iced tea and chocolate cake.

The other three girls grabbed the food and hurried into the kitchen. Debbie called over her shoulder for Jackson to keep Francine still. "We'll bring her a tray."

He watched her devour two helpings of soup, cornbread and lots of iced tea. "Being sick hasn't hurt your appetite."

She threw her napkin at him and ordered him to bring on the dessert. Fancy was even treated to a small bowl of soup to ward off the possibility of getting sick. However, when they refused to give her chocolate cake, she growled at Jackson who said, "That's my cue to leave."

By Thursday, she was stir crazy and though still weak, Francine dressed and went in to work.

Chapter 8

Francine was proud of her secretarial service and had always vowed that she'd work hard and stay independent. She'd been able to make it grow and hated to hear other women voice their ambitions to marry "rich." Thanks to her dedication, she'd succeeded in making her service one of the more profitable small businesses in the area. With planning, savings, smart investments, and the tidy trust from her grandfather, she'd accomplished her goals. This meant that if the man of her dreams came along, she could marry him whether he was rich or not. Her pet peeve was for people to ask, "How's your portfolio?" To which she always answered, "Private." The only two men she would ever depend on financially would be Tony, her financial advisor, and Jack, her accountant. They were honest and hardworking themselves. She had no worry about her portfolio.

The article in the <u>County Magazine</u> proved to be more beneficial than she'd hoped, and several new clients were added during the following week. She kept busy for the next few days leaving little time for daydreaming about Jackson Tanner. It was Thursday evening before Meagan called again.

"Hi Honey. How are you?"

"Not so good. Daddy's missing."

"Missing? Now Meagan, how could he be missing?"

"I can't find him. That's how. Can you come and help me find him?" Her voice quivered.

"Have you called his office?"

"He's not there."

Francine was certain the child was crying, "I'll be right there." She made a quick call to Tanner Enterprises and asked for Jackson's father.

"He's not here right now. I believe he's gone to find Jackson."

Thinking to herself that for once Meagan was not pulling anything, she hurried to the Tanner house. When she arrived, Francine noticed Mrs. Brown backing her car out of the driveway.

Inside, she found Meagan standing at the window with a forlorn look. "Where is Mrs. Brown going?"

"She's going to look for Daddy."

"Now, tell me why you think your daddy is missing."

"He was supposed to be home hours ago, but he never showed up. He's not at his office, and he's not with Grandma and Gramps. He's missing. I know he is. He has a telephone in his car and hasn't called."

"Did you try and call him on his car phone?"

"Of course, I talked to him earlier. He told me he was leaving the office at four and would be home in fifteen minutes and never showed up, and now he doesn't answer." There was a cross of agitation and anxiety in her eyes, so Francine believed her.

"All right. I'll check with the hospitals and police department to see if there's been an accident."

"We can probably wait on that." Meagan said, and she began wringing her hands.

"Well, it won't hurt just to call and see if there has been an accident."

The officer who answered her call said there had been had no accident reported, and a missing person's report could not be filed until twenty-four hours had passed.

"But officer, this is Jackson Tanner we are talking about, and his little girl is frantic."

"Did you say Jackson Tanner? We'll send this right out Ma'am, and we'll see that it's on television." He hung up.

"They're sending out a missing person's report and putting it on television."

"Why?" Meagan said, her eyes stretched wide open.

"Because your daddy is missing, and they became very cooperative when they discovered who he is. Should I call him back and tell him to hold off for a little while?" She had no idea the deputy would go to such extreme that fast. That strange feeling of doubt was creeping into her stomach.

"Uh oh. Maybe they shouldn't put it on television yet?" The little girl paled, and Francine instructed her to sit on the sofa.

Meagan's "uh oh" clinched it. The child's imagination had ballooned again, and this one was serious.

She picked up the telephone to call the police officer again, but a knock at the door interrupted her. Francine hurried to open it. There were two uniformed police officers posted outside, and three plain clothes detectives who hurried inside.

Only one spoke. "Now, Mrs. Tanner, give us all of the details. We're running a report on television which should be on right about now. Where is your daughter?"

Francine turned toward where Meagan had been sitting, but she'd left the room. "I am not Mrs. Tanner, but I'll get Mr. Tanner's daughter."

"Oh?" There goes another raised eyebrow. She sighed and turned to leave the room. "Go ahead," the officer continued speaking, "and I'll turn on the television to see if they've gotten the report out."

"About that report, perhaps we should wait a bit before putting it on television."

"Too late."

The report was on every channel. Meagan was locked in her room.

"Meagan, open this door right now. We need to talk to you."

"I don't feel very well." Meagan said as she opened the door and followed Francine back to where the officers were.

"Now, little lady," asked the older detective. "Don't be afraid. We'll find your daddy. When was the last time you spoke to him?"

Meagan's eyes darted from the officer to the television screen and then to Francine before walking to the couch and sitting down.

"Start from the beginning, Meagan. This is very important." Francine sat beside her and took her hand.

There was a sudden commotion at the door, and all eyes turned to see Jackson attempting to enter the house, with the guard standing by the door holding him back.

"I live here," he shouted as he burst into the room and headed straight to Meagan. She sprang from the sofa and wrapped her arms about his waist.

"I didn't know she was going to put it on television." She pointed toward Francine while sobbing into Jackson's shoulder, as he squatted beside her.

"Put what on television? What the devil's going on here?"

"A missing person's report." Francine shook her head.

"Who's missing?" Jackson turned toward her.

"You are. Well, you were, or that's what we thought." Turning to the child, she added, "That's what I was told, and I fell for it."

The detectives looked perplexed and turned toward Francine as well. She shrugged her shoulders.

"Meagan, what have you done now?" Jackson held his daughter away from him.

"We received a missing person report. When we were told it was Jackson Tanner, we assumed there may be a kidnapping involved, because of your, uh, status. We put it on television and came right over. You wife and little girl were extremely upset. So, where have you been?"

"My wife? I don't have a wife. I've been to the gym. Meagan knew where I'd gone." He scratched his head, and with slumped shoulders, sat on the sofa.

Francine patted him on the shoulder. "Thank goodness you're all right, but when Meagan called me, I checked with your dad's office. Nancy told me he'd gone to look for you. Then when I drove up, Mrs. Brown was leaving. Meagan said *she* was going to look for you. I believed her." Turning her back to the officer, she emphasized, "I did not say I was his wife."

The room became quiet, and the newscaster's voice rang out from the TV, and a picture of a smiling Jackson Tanner flashed across the screen. "This is an emergency report. Jackson Tanner, one of the city's most prominent citizens is missing. His wife believes he may have been kidnapped. The police have put out an all-points bulletin. If you see this man, do not attempt to foil any kidnapping, but contact the police department. The kidnappers may be armed and dangerous."

Francine clutched her head with both hands.

"Oh, my goodness! Get that taken off the news now!" Jackson pressed his face into his hands. The detective jumped at the command, then snapped his fingers and jerked his head toward one of the other men.

"Daddy, I'm sorry."

"Officer, I'm afraid there has been a dreadful mistake."

Mr. & Mrs. Jackson Tanner, Sr. rushed into the house. "Oh, thank goodness, Jackson, you're all right. Did they hurt you? Were they asking for a ransom?" His mother asked.

"Mom. It's Meagan again." Jackson paced the room.

Everyone in the room turned toward the little girl who was crying. These tears were real.

Mr. Tanner stood beside Francine, and she asked him, "Weren't you looking for Jackson? That's what Nancy said when I called your office."

"Sure I was. We went to the gym looking for him so he could sign some papers."

"But, Mrs. Brown went to look for Jackson too?" Her question was directed toward the child. She was beginning to feel as if she were the guilty party.

"She was just going home." Meagan told them. "I'm sorry."

"You lied? Meagan, this is serious. You've alarmed a lot of people here. Whatever possessed you to scare Francine like that?" her grandmother asked.

"She didn't love Fancy, and when she thought Fancy was lost, she started worrying about her, and now she loves the dog."

"The dog?" The detective asked.

Francine nodded.

"Mrs. Tanner. I don't understand what your dog has to do with this?"

"I am not Mrs. Tanner."

"You are not Mrs. Tanner, but Fancy is your dog, and . . . ?"

"And, Fancy was lost at the beach, and I was frantic. I didn't want the dog, but then I got worried, and now I do want the dog."

"What does this have to do with that?" He thrust his hands into the air.

"Meagan, you tell the officer what this has to do with that." Francine mimicked the officer. Her composure was beginning to come back an inch at the time.

"I thought if she heard that Daddy was missing, she would worry about him and start loving him."

It was the harshest tone that she'd ever heard Jackson use with his daughter, "Go to your room right now, young lady. You and I will not talk about this until I calm down."

It was an hour later before the last detective pulled away from the Tanner home after assuring Jackson that no charges would be made against his young daughter. Mrs. Brown had rushed back, after seeing the broadcast. Many of Jackson's friends were calling to express concern. Jackson removed his jacket and sat on the couch, ordering them not to answer the phone again.

Mrs. Brown told him, "I'll stay awhile and answer it. Otherwise, your friends will start coming over, and from the way you look, I don't believe you want a house full of people here."

"You two need to work something out." Mrs. Tanner looked first to Francine then to her son.

"What do you suggest, Mother? A psychiatrist for Meagan - no, I believe I need the psychiatrist. Because I may be losing my mind."

"No." Her voice was firm. "Marriage. Francine needs to be in your life or out of your life." She patted Francine on the arm and said, "I'm sorry Francine."

Mr. Jackson, Sr. who'd remained quiet added his comment. "We like you, Honey, but things are getting out of hand."

"Good night Mother, Dad." He ushered them out, kissing his mother's forehead, and closing the door behind them.

"They're right, you know. I shouldn't have jumped to conclusions, knowing Meagan, but she sounded so convincing. I promise to do everything to sever ties with her. Maybe that will help. They all appear to be blaming me. Perhaps they're right."

"Maybe you should marry me."

Reaching for her sweater, she started toward the door saying, "You'll just have to explain to her that she can't call me anymore . . . What did you say?"

"Marry me."

"Are you crazy?"

"Not yet, but like I told Mother, I may soon be. It won't work."

"It certainly won't work."

"I mean trying to get you out of Meagan's life won't work, and I don't have the mental faculties to fight her any more. She has her heart and mind set on you becoming her mother, so you have to marry me."

"That's about the most romantic proposal a girl ever got. Of course, you're joking."

"I am not joking. Marry me. I'll make it worth your while."

"Oh really now. What are the terms, because if I'm not mistaken, there is a name for that sort of thing?"

"Whatever you want. We get along well. It would make her happy, and she'd stop with this crazy notion of trying to get us together. It really would make your life easier. You could quit your job, if you want."

"So, when will you begin building the ladder?"

"What ladder?"

"The one you'll need when she asks for the moon. You'd better opt for the psychiatrist, because you have lost your mind." Francine pulled on her sweater and stormed from the house.

Her mood had not changed when she slammed the front door at home. All three of the other girls were there at the kitchen table with Mark.

"Now what?" Debbie asked.

"You really should watch television. Of all the nerve. No sirree. I will not marry that man."

Mark rose from the chair and kissed Debbie on the cheek. "I do believe it's time for me to leave. No, don't move, I'll let myself out. I have the gut feeling that this can't wait until tomorrow, and somehow, I don't wish to be involved. You can fill me in on the details."

"Here's your coffee. Now tell us what is going on?" Marcie pushed a steaming cup of coffee toward Francine.

By the time she'd gotten through telling the story, the other three girls were laughing. Each, in turn, expressed their delight that they'd met up with this girl, meaning Meagan, who kept their lives in such a delightful uproar.

"This time, it's not funny. Every time she does something twisted, you three think it's hilarious. This one's the worst." She glared at them and began to pace. She held Fancy so tight, the dog started to whine and squirm in her arms.

"You don't think this entire thing is romantic?" Lillie asked, swooning.

"What could possibly be romantic about it? Hilarious is pushing it. Romantic? No, I don't think so. Sorry, Francine, you're right." Marcie hid a grin behind her hand as she apologized.

"Sounds romantic to me the way this little girl chose her next mother and set her up with her daddy." Lillie persisted.

"She didn't set me up. Remember? I picked him up in a bar. Ever since then, I've been on a collision course. Now, I'm crashing. What am I going to do?"

No one said a word, and Francine stopped pacing and turned to stare at them. "You think I should marry him, don't you?" When they kept silent, she continued, "What is the matter with you idiots? Answer me."

"We, uh, have some things to do upstairs," Debbie said as they brushed past her and hurried from the room. As Fancy began a low growl, she discovered the reason for their hurried exit and pressed her fingers to her temples.

"It was a sorry proposal." Jackson spoke from the doorway. "I apologize."

"What are you doing here? We're severing ties. I'm out of your life. What happened to your discussion with your daughter?" She started pacing again.

"We had an intense discussion about lying. She's grounded for life. I also told her that I proposed to you. She informed me that I should've had a ring and a nice dinner."

"Oh mercy." Francine pressed her fingers against her temples.

"My sister-in-law is there. Heard on the news I was kidnapped. She also agreed that my proposal was not so romantic. It was her idea for me to be here."

"Her idea? Apology accepted. Now git."

"Can't do that. To apologize is not the only reason I came. I came to propose in a more romantic way. Want me to get on my knees or wait until we can have a romantic dinner?"

"If you don't leave, I'll call the police."

"You really think they'd come now?" He laughed.

"Then, I'll let Fancy loose on you."

With that, Jackson reached for the pup and pulled her close, kissing the animal on top of her head. Fancy tilted her tiny head upward and licked Jackson's cheek.

"Traitor."

"Have you had dinner?"

"Thanks to your daughter, I have not."

"Grab your sweater, and let's go for a ride, get a bite to eat. Just something quick, this time. We'll save the romantic dinner date for later. Please?"

"This is the last time. I'll go so we can figure out how to get me out of your life."

Jackson didn't answer but followed her out of the door and to his car. They both looked up toward the upstairs hall window where three pair of eyes peered out. They rode to a small restaurant a few miles away and were seated in the back corner.

"It will work. Listen to what I have to say. Marry me, and give it one year. If you are so unhappy after that year, we can get a divorce."

"An annulment." Francine emphasized.

"Then, you'll do it?"

"I didn't say that, but there's a difference in a divorce and an annulment. An annulment is when you don't, uh, you don't . . ."

"Have sex? We don't have to if you don't want." He reached for her hand.

She snatched her hand away and jerked her head toward him, but before she could say anything, he put his hands up. "OK, OK, Marry me, make Meagan happy and maybe our lives will calm down, and we'll live happy ever after - celibate."

"For just a year, you say?" She twisted her mouth to one side as if in deep thought.

"Then you'll do it? You won't be sorry. We'll have any kind of wedding you want. I'll buy you a car, give you whatever you want."

"I have a car. You're a soft touch, you know, or maybe just touched."

"Well, I do have money. I should spend it to make people I care about happy. It won't be a problem."

"Your soft touch is in your head, Jackson Tanner, not mine. I'm not a gold digger. I have a great business. I love it, and I am independently . . . "

"Wealthy? I know."

"You know? You checked me out?"

He grinned. "Not me. It was Mother, weeks ago." He held his hands up again. "Sorry, but I won't lie about that. Had no idea she was doing it, but she wanted to protect her little boy. Anyway, you're the kind of woman I'd want to marry, kind, pretty, good to my little girl."

"If you were in love, you mean." She told him, while thinking, "I'm madly in love with you despite the fact you aren't in love with me." She'd admitted to herself long ago that she loved Jackson.

He held his head to one side in a vulnerable sort of way, "What are you thinking? Will you marry me?"

"Let me think about it. No. This is absurd."

"But, you just said you'd think about it. Just do that. Here are our hamburgers. Let's eat while you think."

"I believe I'll need a bit longer to think about this."

"All right. Can I tell Meagan you're thinking about it?"

"Oh all right. Yes, I'll marry you. But, I keep my house and my business. My job will not interfere with my relationship with her. Since I'm the boss, I can re-arrange my hours so that I can spend quality time with Meagan. When?"

"We can go to the jewelry store tomorrow and choose a ring. Can't you and Mother get together on the arrangements?" He added. "You're the boss in the entire situation."

"We both know who the boss is in this situation. You want me to call your mother? I can't do that."

"That's O.K. I'll tell her. She'll be delighted."

"Delighted to know her son is marrying a woman he doesn't love in order to please his daughter?"

"Her idea, remember? That's the other thing. Couldn't we at least pretend we're in love?"

"That sounds like a song?" A smile tugged at the corners of her lips. She knew her job would be to pretend to this man that she was not in love. It would be a job because she was in love with him. But she must never let him know. Pretend . . . Pretend.

"So, you'll call your mother, and when she gets in touch with me, I'll pretend."

"You'll have to agree that it will make things simpler if everyone thinks we are in love."

"How will we pull that off?"

"The way you've been kissing me, it shouldn't be difficult."

"The way I've been kissing you . . . you conceited jerk, take me home." She left the booth. He followed with his hands stuck in his pockets, while whistling.

They rode in silence back to her house. She opened the door, and Jackson leaned over and whispered. "Bet if you look close enough, you'll see those upstairs curtains pulled to one side."

"You're right. I'm sure those three pair of eyes are glued to the window. So what?"

"Kiss me."

"I will not."

"If we are going to make this look good you have to kiss me." He pulled her head to him and gave her one of those delicious kisses that she'd longed for the past few weeks.

He broke the kiss, made a fist and touched it to her chin. "I don't believe it's going to be too difficult to fool anybody, do you?"

"You are a jerk!" She slammed the car door and hurried inside. Debbie, Marcie and Lillie met her at the front door.

"Well?" They asked in unison.

Francine didn't slow her pace, but upon reaching the top of the stairs, she turned to face them, "Wanna be in my wedding?"

They had already started following her, and she couldn't make it to her room in time to lock the door. They were right behind her with Fancy in tow. No one slept that night, and by early morning, one fabulous wedding was planned down to the last rose petal, subject to the approval of her future mother-in-law and, of course, her daughter to be. Debbie would be Maid of Honor; Jackson's sister-in-law would be Matron of Honor; Marcie, Lillie and Jackson's nieces would be bridesmaids. They assumed that Jackson's dad or brother would be best man, and of course, Mark must be an usher along with Francine's own brother. Since Jackson's brother, Travis, was serving out of the country in the US Air Force, she was not sure he would even be able to get leave to come for the wedding.

"What will Meagan do in the wedding?" Marcie asked.

"Whatever the heck she wants." They fell back on the bed laughing.

It was early the following afternoon that Jackson poked his head into the doorway of her office. "I'll pick you up about seven tonight for dinner. That all right with you?"

"Sure, but I'm kind of sleepy. We'll have to make it an early night." She didn't realize how that sounded until she heard giggles behind her.

Grinning, he closed the door, leaving her to make the explanations. Francine decided that giving the news to her family about the marriage would have to wait until she had an engagement ring on her finger. Then, they could meet Jackson. It still didn't seem real, and she hadn't quite figured out how she was going to convince everyone else she loved Jackson while pretending to Jackson that she didn't love him.

He'd made arrangements for the jeweler to stay open late for them one evening so they would not be disturbed as they chose the rings. Jackson bumped the tray of jewels causing diamonds to scatter everywhere. It took thirty minutes for the owner to find them all and return them to their proper case. She settled on a solitaire diamond, nothing too elegant, but fit her idea of being just right. Later that evening, as they dined, Jackson spilled a glass of wine and stumbled when they left the restaurant. Over the next few weeks, a strange twist of events took place. Francine became the calm one while Jackson turned into a nervous wreck.

Plans for the wedding went along well, and soon Jackson and Francine drove to her family's home where Jackson proceeded to enchant everyone.

When the wedding day arrived, Francine's mother helped with her dress, exclaiming how beautiful she looked. Lillie was thirty minutes late and came wearing the wrong shoes.

When she started to cry, Francine shushed her, declaring that they would all walk down the aisle barefoot. "It will be perfect."

Meagan came to say that her daddy could not find the wedding rings.

"Remind him that your grandfather is best man, and the best man has my ring, and Debbie has his ring."

With the guests seated, Francine peeked into the sanctuary in time to see Jackson walk out, followed by Meagan who'd insisted on helping her grandfather serve as best man. She'd refused to be a flower girl. Jackson stumbled, and the preacher caught him.

Lillie walked down the aisle first, followed by Marcie, Brenda's daughters, Brenda Tanner, then Debbie.

Francine's daddy smiled down at her and whispered, "This is the beginning of a journey, my dear. I pray you'll always be happy. Are you happy, Francine?"

"Yes, Daddy." It wasn't a complete lie. The journey had begun when she'd had a rendezvous with a perfect stranger she picked up in a bar. She would not share some details of her life with her daddy. The pianist began playing, "Here Comes the Bride," and she squeezed her father's arm as they walked down the aisle. The ceremony was well underway and at the appropriate time, Mr. Tanner, Sr. attempted to hand the ring to Jackson who dropped it. Meagan scrambled to retrieve it and shouted, "Here it is, Daddy."

The guests laughed. Jackson blushed. He took the ring from his daughter, and his hands shook as he placed it on the finger of his bride. Debbie handed her Jackson's ring, and the deed was almost done.

There was excitement at the back of the church, and all eyes turned to see a dashing man in a United States Air Force uniform enter. The Matron of Honor and three junior Bridesmaids rushed toward him. After hugs all around, the ecstatic group turned toward Jackson and Francine who motioned for them to join them. All five marched up front, and the pianist began playing God Bless America, and everyone stood and sang.

The minister ended the ceremony with, "I now pronounce you husband and wife and one big happy family. And, all of God's people said . . ."

The entire congregation shouted, "Amen!"

As unusual as it was, the ceremony was beautiful, seeming to end much too soon. Francine tossed the bouquet over her shoulder toward twenty hopeful young ladies. It landed in the hands of Debbie, who shared a smile with Mark.

Over three hundred guests attended the ceremony and reception, and Francine thought the line of well-wishers was never ending. She and Jackson were happy to share the limelight with the handsome Captain Travis Tanner, who stood beaming at all of their family and friends. The smiling couple waited as long as possible before leaving for the airport. They hugged everyone goodbye and climbed into the waiting limousine.

They flew to Barbados, and when they arrived at the hotel, a friendly and attentive staff member greeted them with a welcome beverage. They said "no" to the jet-lag massage, and upon arrival at the honeymoon suite, they discovered that it had a fantastic view of the ocean. There was a cool ambience, accented with a décor of immaculate white walls and curtains that sparkled with blue accents. The rooms held mahogany furniture with rattan covering on floors of terracotta tile. A pale marble bathroom featured twin sinks, a large shower area and a Jacuzzi. The staff member showed them their private balcony with an outside Jacuzzi. He told them that they "would be wrapped in luxury from the fine white linens and goose-down comforters. Each suite is equipped with a minibar, refrigerator and espresso machine."

During their three-week stay, the weather was perfect, and Jackson anticipated and catered to every possible desire that Francine could have. During the day, they enjoyed scuba diving instructions, excursions, parasailing and glass-bottom boat trips.

Water taxis and beach shuttles transported them to area facilities, and they visited as many of the breathtaking natural wonders possible, taking enough pictures to fill several albums. They purchased so many souvenirs, they had to buy extra luggage to carry them home. Everyone who saw them could only imagine them to be the happiest couple alive - enjoying a honeymoon of perfection. It was . . . until they retired to their suite for the evening. When they were alone, they barely spoke and avoided touching each other. At night, Jackson slept on the sofa, leaving Francine to get lost in the king-sized bed with silk linens. She refused to cry.

Chapter 9

This marriage was not as easy as Francine had thought it would be. Her things had been placed in Jackson's bedroom. Because Meagan watched their every move, the two of them agreed to sleep in the same bed. Jackson assured her in a polite way she'd have nothing to worry about. The king-sized bed was still too small for two people bent on avoiding contact. The first morning Francine awoke to find herself snuggled in Jackson's arms with his face pressed into her hair. That evening she carefully arranged two pillows between them. Fancy had taken up with Meagan and Taffy, and for the most part ignored Jackson and Francine, so the pillows were the only thing separating them.

During the next few weeks, Francine could not fault Jackson in his attitude or conduct toward her whenever someone else was present. Alone in the bedroom was a different story. He avoided physical contact, and his conversation with Francine was almost hostile.

Francine kept her secretarial business, but worked only until Meagan came home from school each day. Whatever she planned for the three of them worked with precision, and with the Christmas season close in hand, she was busy with preparations. Francine thought she would make it. But, after three months of pretending to pretend, it began to tell on her, and by Christmas Eve, she crashed.

Looking into the mirror without makeup, the dark circles

beneath her eyes were evident. She started to cry. Jackson found her sobbing into her pillow.

"I can't do this anymore. We have to end this."

"I know." He agreed.

One thing was certain, she could no longer lie beside this man she loved without so much as a touch. At first, she had put herself to sleep by imagining how it would be to have him make love to her, but that tactic proved to be more frustrating.

"I'm sorry, Jackson. I didn't think it would be so difficult."

"Nor I. There now. Don't cry anymore." Jackson pulled her to him. He wore soft, silk pajamas, and his light aftershave smelled fresh and clean.

She didn't really mean to, but couldn't help herself and snuggled closer, safe in the comfort of his arms. Within seconds, his lips were on hers, and their passionate lovemaking was more wonderful than she'd ever imagined. Afterwards, Francine fell asleep in Jackson's arms.

When she awoke the next morning, Jackson had already removed himself from the bed and was at the breakfast table alone, his mood a drastic change from that of the previous night. His conversation was crisp and curt.

"I'm sorry about last night." He snapped. "I promise it won't happen again."

She could not believe the attitude change from the previous evening. His words pierced her heart as if they had sharp blades. She gasped and ran from the room. It was Christmas morning making it impossible to hide for long. Francine emerged when the other members of his family arrived, which included his brother and sister-in-law with their girls and the senior Tanners. The women put the final touches to the holiday dinner, and no one seemed to notice the tension between Jackson and Francine. Meagan was ecstatic as she and her cousins swam in Christmas wrapping paper and ribbon. Each girl received porcelain dolls, several outfits, and jewelry. Fancy, who'd gotten lost a couple of times in the middle of everything, enjoyed her rawhide bones, a red sweater and a shiny new bowl. Taffy, in her new collar, eyed everyone with suspicion from her spot on the back of a chair. At least, it was apparent that she'd made the right choices in shopping for Jackson. Her gifts to him included clothes, but the rare edition of a book he'd been looking for brought him obvious pleasure. He gave her a pinkie ring that held several tiny rubies. Francine couldn't hide her pleasure and caught glimpses of him gazing at her. The remainder of the day went by with no apparent strain.

True to his word, he didn't allow a repeat of the night before. The first night was not as difficult as she'd expected because she was exhausted, but they woke entwined in each other's arms. Each night thereafter, Jackson placed a heavy comforter on the floor beside the bed for himself, and each night, it took longer for Francine to fall asleep. She found no comfort in the fact that Jackson seemed to be having the same difficulty.

By the end of February, Jackson announced that he would be away for two weeks on a business trip, indicating in a vague way that it had something to do with the merger. She was hurt that he had not even suggested she accompany him. Francine wondered if he'd gone alone.

If Francine had thought she was miserable with Jackson in the house, the evenings and nights without him were unbearable. Her imagination ran wild because the dreams of Jackson also had a woman in a red dress. She pushed Francine farther and farther away until Francine found herself sitting at the end of a long table. Even during the nights that she slept well, Francine was as tired when she got out of bed each morning as when she pulled the covers over her in the evening. Something was wrong, dreadfully wrong, and when Mrs. Brown questioned her, she blamed it on restlessness with Jackson being away. When Jackson returned, she told him of her decision to take a leave of absence from her business and visit with her family and was surprised at his response.

"That would be best for you. You haven't had any time off, and you haven't seen your family since the wedding."

"You sound as if this is a job."

"Isn't it?" He was sarcastic in his quick response, and he turned and left the room.

She drove the three hours to her parents' home the following day. Meagan moped. Jackson spent more time away from home, and Mrs. Brown merely sighed.

"Is she coming back?" Meagan asked one evening as he was preparing to go out.

"Sure she is, Honey."

"I thought she'd be happy married to us."

"She is very happy being your mother."

"Is she happy being your wife?"

He stared down at his vulnerable daughter. "You wait here a minute, and let me make a call. I've decided to spend the evening with my favorite girl. You go pick a book, and I'll read to you."

Jackson went into his den, canceled his plans and the baby-sitter and returned to his daughter.

"All right, now, what's it going to be? Alice in Wonderland?"

"No, daddy. Could we just sit here and talk?"

"My, you do sound grown up. What do you want to talk about?"

"Francine."

"I was afraid of that."

"Daddy, what's wrong with Francine? Do you think she'll go to the doctor while she's away?"

"Nothing's wrong with her, Honey. She just needed to get away for a while. Needed a visit with her parents. She'll be back soon." He placed his arms around her.

Meagan straightened, "If she wasn't sick, then why was she puking every morning?"

"Why was she what?"

"Puking. Every morning, she puked."

"Can you stop using that word?"

"What word?"

"Puking."

"How can I tell you she was puking if I don't use the word?" Jackson sighed. "Go ahead. What else?"

"She always cried after she did it."

"Cried?"

"Yes, *Daddy*, she cried."

"Meagan, how long had this been going on before she left?" Jackson was sitting on the edge of the sofa with his hands placed on her shoulders.

"I don't know, days, weeks, why don't you ask Mrs. Brown? She saw her puking too."

"Meagan, is this another one of your tricks?"

"Tricks? I don't play tricks anymore. Not since you and Francine got married. That's what I wanted. I didn't mean to make her sick and unhappy."

"Well, Honey. That's the problem. Neither of us wanted to make her sick or unhappy."

"She doesn't want us? Doesn't she want to be my mommy?"

"She wants you with all her heart."

"Doesn't she want you?"

"Meagan, I guess you must know. Francine married me to make you happy. She isn't in love with me." He signed. "It was sort of a deal."

"She does love you – don't you love her?"

"Of course, I love her very much. Francine told you she loves me to make you happy."

"Then why did she walk around all goo goo eyes when you were around? She blushed all the time when you hugged her."

"It's time for you to go to bed young lady. We'll talk more tomorrow."

With his daughter tucked in, Jackson hurried back to the telephone and dialed Mrs. Brown.

"Were you aware that Francine had been sick and throwing up?"

"Yes, weren't you?"

"No, I wasn't. Why didn't you tell me?"

"Mr. Tanner. I work for you, and I don't want to anger you, but for a man who heads up a big corporation, you sure are a dummy."

"Why can't you just speak plain English and tell me what is wrong with my wife?"

"For one thing, you've been a real jerk toward that pretty young thing. That didn't make her throw up. How she got in her condition with the way you treat her, I'll never know. You have some bad attitude."

"What condition?"

"You really don't know, do you? You figure." Mrs. Brown replaced the telephone onto the receiver.

He stood with his mouth open and murmured to himself, "She couldn't be. But then again, it only takes one time. Oh my, I am a jerk."

Grabbing the portable phone, he dialed Mrs. Brown again while running to his room and started piling clothes into a suitcase. "Mrs. Brown, you have to come over and stay with Meagan."

"And, where do you think you are going this time of night?"

"Let's just say that I figured it out."

"I'll be right there."

He made the three-hour drive in two, lucky not to have been pulled by a patrol officer. It was eleven P. M. The lights were still on in her parents' house, but Jackson could not make himself go to that door. He decided that a new day would make for a better start in pleading his case. Groveling would be more like it.

Jackson waited an entire day before working up the nerve to knock on her parents' door. That's when he learned Meagan had called to find out if he was there. Francine had become alarmed when he had not arrived. She'd panicked when she couldn't reach him on his cell phone, packed her things and headed home, or at least to the Tanner residence. She hadn't quite become accustomed to the idea that it was her home.

"Jackson, you poor dear." Her mother met him at the door. "C'mon in."

"I need to see Francine in private, please?"

She told him, "When Meagan telephoned this morning, we became alarmed that you never arrived. Where were you?"

"In a motel. Couldn't get the nerve to face Francine."

"It's time for you two to work this out. She loves you very much, you know."

"No, I don't know. She has spent a great deal of time and effort since we met trying to convince me otherwise."

"And, you've done the same? Look Jackson, Francine is my daughter, and I love her."

"She confided in you then? I didn't want to pressure her. Meagan was doing enough of that. My intentions were good."

"Young man, haven't you heard that the road to torment is paved with good intentions? Yes, in answer to your question, she told me everything."

"Yes, I've heard that saying from my mother many times. Now, don't I know it. Being married to Francine and not being able to show her how much I love her has been pure torment."

"That's not all your fault. Don't beat yourself up anymore. Go home. She'll be waiting for you. You take good care of my little girl and my grandchild."

He nodded and hurried to his car only to find that he was out of gas. An hour later, with the tank filled, Jackson was on his way. There had been an accident on the freeway, which detained him another two hours. On his way again, the car began to jerk and bump. Another hour later, with tire changed, he was again on his way. This time the three-hour drive took six. Meagan met him at the door.

"Oh daddy, where have you been? Francine was here looking for you. Why didn't you answer your cell phone?"

"Was here? Why did she leave? I was in such a hurry; I forgot to plug it into the charger."

"You didn't come, and I called her mom who said you'd been there and left, so she went back looking for you."

"Back?" One hour into the drive back to the Bruckner home, he noticed Francine's car on the other side of the median headed in the opposite direction.

"Oh no!" Frantic, he hurried to the next exit and was in hot pursuit of her red Thunderbird. He dialed his home number.

"Meagan. If Francine comes back there. Tell her to stay put. I don't even know her cell phone number. If you have it, tell me."

"Where are you, daddy, and what is that noise?"

"A siren." Fifteen minutes later, he collected his ticket and once again was on his way.

Francine met him at the door. "You look exhausted."

"You look pregnant."

"Are you angry?"

"I wasn't angry when we got pregnant, was I? Why didn't you tell me you really loved me?"

"How do you know I love you?"

"Everybody told me."

"Jackson, I love you, and I really want to be your wife. You didn't act like you loved me. You never told me."

"Francine, I love you, and I really want to be your husband."

"Geez, it sure has been a job getting you two together." Meagan squeezed between the two of them.

"And, you did a grand job of it. Not your fault that we are such slow movers." Jackson told her.

"Now, all I need is a little sister or brother."

They assured her that they had also taken care of that detail, and they sent their cupid daughter to bed.

Soon after, they crawled into the king-sized bed and fell asleep with Jackson's arms wrapped about Francine, one hand resting on her stomach.

Francine was up and out of the door soon after Jackson left for the office. He'd promised to take care of a few things and return in a couple of hours. She instructed Mrs. Brown to let Meagan sleep late since it was Saturday. Besides, she wanted to see her former housemates before they scattered for the day, have a cup of coffee with them, and tell them the good news. This was one baby that would have three godmothers.

There were squeals, hugs and a good bit of jumping about from the others. Francine told them she'd better wait a bit on the jumping, since the morning sickness hadn't gone away yet. They insisted that breakfast was the one meal she needed. However, instead of her usual eggs, they gave her sweet oatmeal with a softened banana, toast, and a glass of milk.

Francine missed the sisterly contact with her best friends, but wouldn't trade her life now. Besides, they assured her that they were only minutes away.

After eating a good breakfast and not feeling queasy, she told them. "I know you ladies have a lot to do, and I have to run by the bank. Since today is Saturday, they'll only be open until twelve Noon. I need to order some checks and transfer money."

Lillie asked, "Are you going to the branch next to my cell phone company?"

"Sure, whatcha need?"

"My battery is dead, won't charge. Could you pick me up a new battery? I have a ten o'clock hair appointment and won't have time to go by."

"No problem. Give me the phone and not just the battery. They can check it out, see if the phone itself is all right, and I'll be sure to get the right battery."

Lillie tossed the phone to Francine and was out the front door. She said goodbye to the other girls and was on her way, leaving them deep into planning a baby shower, although the baby would not be here until September.

When she arrived at the bank, she noticed only two other

cars in the parking lot, but the cell phone place looked busy. She murmured to herself, "I'll do the banking first."

She left the car and entered the bank. Three men followed behind her, one by himself carrying a toolbox, and the other two soon afterward. The man with the toolbox announced to Melody, one of the tellers, that he'd come to check out the alarm system.

"No one told me anybody was coming." Melody said.

"Well, George called me at home last night. Said there may be a problem."

"All right, come on back." He went around the counter and busied himself while the other two men stood at the center counter as if filling out deposit slips.

The man behind the counter reached over to pull the shade at the drive-through.

Melody asked, "What are you doing?" She reached for the telephone.

The man told her firmly, "Don't even think about it." He proceeded to snatch all of the telephones from the receptacles and tossed them to one of the other men, who shouted, "All right, do what we say, and nobody gets hurt."

They all produced guns, and one of the other men who appeared to be in his early twenties asked, "Did you get the alarm off?"

"Sure I did." The man grinned. "I know my business."

The third man instructed Francine and the other two customers to hand over their cell phones. The male customer had one on his belt, and the other girl pulled hers from her purse. Francine reached into her purse and pulled out Lillie's cell phone, and the man jerked it from her hand. She hadn't been surprised that there were only two other customers this time of morning, but wondered why there were only two tellers present and none of the men.

Two of the robbers filled canvas bags with money and helped themselves to more from the safe, which stood wide open. The younger man kept his gun pointed at the five people who now huddled together.

It was the older man who announced, "Now, we're going to leave this building. No one follows, and you can't call anyone or set off any alarms since they don't work. See, you've all been good little troopers, so you won't get hurt."

Francine had kept quiet, though her heart pounded. Even under pressure, her memory had always been excellent. A stickler for specifics, she took in as much detail about the three men as she could.

As soon as they left the bank, she reached into her purse and pulled out her own cell phone and dialed 911.

Melody rushed to where Francine stood, "Leave it to you, Francine, to carry two cell phones."

"My name is Francine Tanner." She spoke into the phone. "I'm at Southeast Bank on Treadmill Road. It's just been robbed. There were three men, one about forty-five with a graying beard, one about thirty, clean shaven, and a young boy in his early twenties with long blond hair. They all wore caps, blue jeans, and one has on a red shirt." She continued to speak as she peered out the window. "They're pulling out of the lot now in a metallic green Chevrolet and are heading North on Treadmill Road."

She listened to the dispatcher before continuing, "No, you can't call back here. They pulled the phones and cut the lines, and one of them turned off the alarm. No, this is not a hoax. You need to quit wasting time and get moving, Buster."

"Honey." The dispatcher told her, "Help is already on the way."

Melody hugged her smiling, but the new young teller was crying. Before Francine could hang up, they heard sirens blaring, and she asked Melody, "Where are all the men and other tellers?"

"They're in a meeting upstairs." They turned to see the others hurrying down the stairs to the lobby. They'd heard the sirens.

Within ten minutes, the parking lot was filled with police

cars, and officers streamed into the bank. Francine thought she'd merely blinked and there they were.

"Who is Francine?" One of the officers asked.

"Me, and I need to sit. Now."

"Yep, you sure do, you're mighty pale lady. Do I know you?"

She recognized him as one of the officers who had been at the Jackson home on the night Meagan reported her daddy missing. He nodded.

"Oh yeah, I remember now. Are you always in the middle of chaos?" He smiled.

"Looks like I am."

"Well, this time, it's a good thing. Looka' here at what we got." She saw several other officers escorting the three robbers, wearing handcuffs, into the bank.

They glared at Francine as she explained to the officer how she ended up with an extra cell phone. "When they had asked for our cell phones, I pulled out Lillie's phone with the dead battery and handed it over."

"Good thinking, Ma'am. Looks like this time, you're the hero. Want me to call your husband, uh, Mr. Tanner?" The policeman was embarrassed as his eyes lowered to her stomach.

"Oh no, does he have to know? Yes, now, he's my husband."

"I think so. You're really looking kind of puny."

As he reached out to her, she turned toward the waste basket and lost every bit of the wonderful breakfast she'd had earlier. Melody ran to fetch some paper towels.

One of the men from the bank commented, "We heard sirens – had no idea . . ."

The police officer who was interviewing Francine took her cell phone and pressed the speed dial for Jackson's home. He spoke with Mrs. Brown who had assured him that Mrs. Tanner's husband would be there right away.

Soon, she heard a ruckus and looked up to see two police

officers attempting to restrain Jackson who yelled at them, "That's my wife. Get out of my way."

The young policeman who'd called her home told them, "It's all right. That's our hero's husband." He seemed to delight in calling her a hero.

After being told the details, he said, "Francine, what were you thinking? Are you all right?"

"Hey, don't fuss at her." The officer touched Jackson on the arm. "She's our hero."

Jackson's alarmed look caused him to step back. "Young man, this is my wife. Come on Francine."

"Where are you taking her? She needs to come to the station and give us a statement."

"She's going to see a doctor. Don't you have your crooks? Any statement she gives will have to wait."

"Sure thing, Mr. Tanner. We'll need to talk to her soon though. She's our main witness. She saved the day."

Melody and the other employees who knew Francine came over with big hugs. "Can we come see you later?" The new girl, who'd been taken aside for questioning, was still crying and clinging to the young robber, which explained a lot.

Jackson looked at them and realized how frightened Melody and the other customers must have been. He was thankful that his coolheaded wife had been there. "Sure, you can. Call her later this afternoon. She will have rested, and I'm sure you'll all feel better when you talk, but right now, I have to get her to a doctor."

"You think I need a doctor?" Francine asked.

Jackson had his arm tight around her. He stopped at the door, turned back to see that everyone had their eyes fixed on the two of them and announced; "Sure, she needs a doctor. We're gonna have a baby."

Chapter 10

By early spring, several things had become obvious. Meagan would have a brother *and* a sister, or two of the same. A sonogram had proven there were two babies. Romance had moved along with Debbie and Mark. There would be another wedding in the near future. Mrs. Butler, who'd gone to Florida to be with her sick son, had no knowledge of the wedding or the pregnancy. Francine felt a mixture of relief and apprehension and wondered if she would ever get past Mrs. Butler's accusing eye on her return to church.

Jackson wondered aloud as to what kind of challenge they would have with two more children. Would they be like Meagan? The nursery would be across the hall from the master bedroom. Francine busied herself looking at paint, curtains and ordering doubles of all the basics. They had the room painted a pale yellow with a Noah's ark border as a chair rail, giving it the final touch. No decision was made without Meagan's approval.

They decided to wait until the births to learn whether there would be a boy and a girl, or two girls or two boys. With no preference, they were sure whatever the combination, they would be ecstatic. Everyone wanted to pamper her. She didn't think that she could ever get used to it. In fact, it was difficult sometimes to remain calm about it.

Though her secretarial service was thriving, Francine admitted it would not be possible for her to continue to work with three children. Lillie and Marcie became partners and purchased the business from Francine. They insisted she keep a small interest so they could call on her for advice.

Debbie came over as often as possible and sure enough, soon announced there'd be a June wedding and asked Francine to be her Matron of Honor.

"I'm so fat." She wrinkled her face and after only a few moments, she accepted. "Yes, Debbie, you know I'm honored, but I won't be a pretty one. Are you sure you don't want to wait until October when my body might be on its way back to normal?"

"You will, as always, be lovely. No, I will not wait. So be thinking about colors for your dress as well as those of Lillie and Marcie. I want you to decide on them."

"That's only a month away, and I have no idea how big I'll be, but from the looks of my tummy now, I'll need an extra, triple X, large, huge . . ."

"Now, Francine, don't exaggerate. Let's just pick out the colors and the style, then the seamstress can get busy on the bridesmaid dresses. She'll just have to whip yours up at the last minute." They giggled as they always had, happy their relationship had grown, not deteriorated, since Francine's marriage. Even Jackson had insisted the girls have free run of the house and had declared them to be his new sisters.

It was a large house, even more elaborate than the beach house, but the comfortable den was the center of most activity. In one corner stood a game table used for chess and card games. A grand piano graced the other end of the room where Meagan practiced daily. Francine looked forward to winter when they could have a nice warm fire in the massive fireplace which was encased by rustic stones. On the opposite side of the room was a long elegant bar with lots of stools for company. The French doors opened to the patio outside where a picnic table waited for the times when the whole crew could be together.

Francine looked around the room admiring everything until Debbie's voice broke into her thoughts.

"Now, back to my wedding."

"Sorry, my mind drifted for a moment. What about Meagan?" Both women realized her young ears were pressed against the door, listening. They decided to play along.

"You know," said Debbie, "if it hadn't been for Meagan getting you to be her pretend Mom, I'd have continued to pester you about dating Mark, and there would have been a different outcome. It helped that you didn't fulfill your intentions to murder Jackson that day when you went to his home, after you'd mistaken him for Mark. Even so, I'm not sure Meagan would be interested in being a junior bridesmaid at my wedding." Debbie winked at Francine.

"I will. I will." That was the response they expected. Meagan hadn't meant to let them know she was listening, but when Francine and Debbie laughed at her so hard, she realized they'd known all along.

"You knew I was listening, didn't you?"

"Of course, Honey. We knew you were eavesdropping. Nothing gets past you anyway. Better work on that because you may sometimes hear something you don't want to hear." Francine smiled as she repeated her own grandmother's warning.

Quick to change the subject and offer her advice, Meagan said, "I think pale rose would be the perfect color, especially in the summer." She added. "It will be so cool."

The older girls laughed again, knowing the child was well on her way to taking over the event.

"Just don't make it green. I'm not sick in the morning any more, but I can't stand the thought of green." Francine offered.

"Mom." Meagan loved calling her that. "You can't stand the thought of breakfast since the robbery, or coffee for that matter. Now, you keep eating all the saltines we try to save for Katie."

"I know, that tiny bit of salty taste soothes my tummy. My love for coffee will return, just not yet."

Over the next few weeks, Debbie and her two housemates completed the preparations, all subject to Meagan's approval. She'd insisted the wedding take place in the Tanner home, and on a beautiful day in late June, Debbie became Mrs. Mark Johnson. Despite her weight gain, Francine was pleased with the way she looked. The pale rose color, chosen by Meagan, was perfect for each of the two bridesmaids and one junior bridesmaid. Meagan, who'd unofficially been assistant director of everything, announced she would be a wedding planner when she grew up.

"What happened to your working with animals?"

"Can't I do that too?"

Everyone assured her that being a wedding planner would be a great profession but wondered if Meagan would ever understand that she would not be able to choose the brides for the grooms or vice-versa . . .

Mark's best man was Jackson Tanner, and all of the Tanner family attended the wedding, including Jackson's parents and his brother's clan. The wedding was beautiful, not quite on the grand scale as Jackson and Francine's, but wonderful all the same. Debbie had no close family, except her grandparents, but the Tanner family had declared that they'd adopted all four of the girls.

Lillie and Danny, Dr. Best's tech, had become quite the couple as well as Marcie and Charlie, the Tanner Building guard who'd witnessed Francine's elevator episode. He was at the end of one of the rows as the attendants passed by and gave Francine a knowing wink. No doubt, those four stood in line to be Meagan's next projects.

Francine settled in a soft chair and thought about the many changes in her life since she first met Jackson. Now, she was married, moved, expecting twins and had sold her business. She'd been reluctant to sell her home because it had belonged to Grandmother Mailey. However, Mark persuaded her to allow him and Debbie to purchase it. The clincher was when he insisted that the other two girls continue to live there until they married.

Debbie had said, "The house is much too big for the two of us, but it's home to all three of us, and it holds so many wonderful memories. Mark and I will be happy to raise a family there." She blushed.

Mark squeezed her hand, saying, "It would be foolish to have Lillie and Marcie change their entire lifestyle because we're the owners. With the three of you close at hand, I'll be able to call on you from time to time, in case I can't handle Debbie." He'd teased, receiving a playful punch in the stomach.

The couple returned from changing into travel clothes. Debbie wore tan slacks, a short-sleeved blouse with yellow roses against a background of pale green leaves, and sandals. Mark also wore tan slacks with a sky blue shirt that matched his eyes. The happy couple would spend their first night as a married couple at the beach house before leaving for a short honeymoon in Barbados, a gift from the Tanner family.

They seemed to be delaying their departure until an impatient Meagan said, "Good grief, I thought once married, the couple was anxious to get away to be alone."

Mark laughed as he corrected her. "Eager is the word, anxious means you're worried."

"Then if you are eager, go." Meagan told them. After another round of hugs, they were off.

Since the merger was such a success and Jackson's brother, Travis, had fully retired from the Air Force, he was taking more of an on-hands position with the business. This enabled Jackson to spend extra time with Francine and Meagan.

Summer continued to be hot. July and August were record breakers. With her fingers, ankles and toes swollen, Francine only ventured outside after the sun slipped behind the trees. She didn't wear shoes about the house, and rings were out of the question.

Jackson, Meagan and Mrs. Brown were frustrating her because of their constant pampering. If she so much as grunted, Fancy was by her side with a questioning look until assured that Francine was all right.

The doctor had ordered her to spend as much time as she could stand, in bed. She insisted that the sofa in the den was a close second during the day, and the doctor allowed her that request.

"Allow her, my foot," exclaimed Mrs. Brown. That independent thing does as she pleases." All the while, she was pulling over an ottoman for Francine to prop her feet.

She'd assumed that September 24; nine months from Christmas Eve, to be the obvious due date, but it came and went. Meagan became more and more eager. Jackson had in secret, initiated the help of her look-a-like cousin, Tammy, who became her constant companion. Her job was to keep Meagan occupied so Francine would be relieved from worrying about her and vice-versa. Jackson realized that so much attention, with Meagan's persistence in fluffing her pillows and asking what she could do, was making his wife more nervous. Meagan still looked daily at the pictures in the books that the doctor had given them and wanted to keep track of how much the babies had grown. No one could keep her from going with Francine to the doctor, and she was present at each sonogram.

Tammy was only a few months older than her cousin, Meagan, but had all but moved into the Tanner home. She was determined to do her job well. She reminded her when it was time to practice piano and played chess and other games with her. Francine felt that she'd not have survived otherwise, but she did enjoy it when the two girls took turns brushing her hair and giving her foot rubs. Only at bedtime, did she move to their room upstairs. Fancy's affection toward Francine had returned, and she slept at Francine's feet.

One of the highlights of Fancy's life was when Shirley brought

Katie over for a visit. Fancy seemed to know that Katie had saved her life. Mrs. Brown always made sure to serve them saltines.

One Saturday afternoon, Fancy and Katie were out back with Mrs. Brown. Shirley and the very pregnant lady were in the den chatting. The two young girls were on the floor in front of the coffee table working a jigsaw puzzle. Jackson was in his study paying bills.

Mrs. Brown had already brought in iced tea and cookies, instructing Francine to keep her intake to a minimum. The doorbell jarred them from their comfortable state, and the girls jumped up to answer it but Francine told them, "Stay put. I'll get it." She didn't want to move, however, she knew it would be best for her in the end. "I'll be right back, Shirley."

She opened the door to face Mrs. Butler whose eyes wandered over her painfully swollen body.

After a snobbish grunt, she said, "I understand that Mr. Tanner has volunteered to serve on the finance committee at the church, and I've brought over the records."

"And, how are you Mrs. Butler? I didn't realize you'd returned from Florida. How's your son?"

"He's all better now." She appeared to soften her tone a bit at the mention of her son. "He's recovered from the injuries he received in the accident."

"I'm sorry, didn't know he'd been in an accident. Was just told he was ill. Come right in, and I'll get Jackson."

She left the room to find her husband, relieved to get away from Mrs. Butler's scrutiny. Before the visitor stepped inside, Meagan had left the den to check on Katie and Fancy, leaving Tammy and Shirley there.

Shirley attempted conversation, but Mrs. Brown turned to Tammy and asked, "Well, how are you young lady?"

"I'm fine." She didn't realize that Mrs. Butler mistook her for her cousin.

"I see that Francine is still living here?" It was a statement more than a question.

"Yes Ma'am. Isn't it wonderful? She's going to have twins. I think they know what they are but won't say."

"So, she finally married your daddy?"

"Oh no Ma'am. She isn't married to my daddy."

"Well, we'll see who'll be serving on my committee." With that, Mrs. Butler clenched the papers to her chest and stormed from the house.

Shirley and Tammy were was appalled at the woman's attitude but not privy to the circumstances leading up to her hasty departure. Nor did they know why Meagan, who'd returned in time to see Mrs. Butler leave, thought it was so funny.

By the time Francine reached Jackson, she doubled over with pain, and he shouted for Meagan.

It was Meagan who made the call to the doctor and to Francine's parents who were on standby. It was Meagan who called her grandparents, Tammy's parents and Debbie, Lillie and Marcie.

Shirley instructed Jackson to bring the car to the front door while she assisted Francine.

"Shouldn't we call the ambulance?" Jackson asked.

"I don't think so. You still have time. Drive at a safe speed. Meagan seems to have everything in hand here. I'll check with you later." Shirley waved them off and called for Katie. Mrs. Brown would take care of Fancy and Taffy, who'd always appeared unconcerned about the chaotic activities of the household. She'd become accustomed to the chaos that took place from time to time in the Tanner home. No doubt two more members of the family would not affect her one way or the other.

Several hours later, there was no sign of babies being born, but the waiting room was filled with family and friends. Debbie, Lillie and Marcie had arrived, each taking turns sitting with their friend, helping with her breathing exercises. They decided that the nervous father would be useless in the delivery room. Jackson Michael Tanner, III and Melody Laura Tanner arrived, each weighing in at six pounds.

When Francine remembered to ask about Mrs. Butler, Meagan delighted in telling them about the conversation the woman had with Tammy and her stormy exit from the house.

Jackson called her right away and gave her a condensed update on the happenings at the Tanner household while she'd been away. He promised a full explanation as soon as they brought the babies home. Only after Meagan was convinced that she could visit first thing next morning, did she agree to leave. With a final round of hugs and congratulations, everyone cleared the hospital room, leaving Jackson and Francine alone with their precious new arrivals.

They swapped the babies back and forth until the nurse came in to take them to the nursery.

Jackson scratched his head and said, "I don't want to discourage our pleasure, but what in the world can we expect from our eldest child? You do realize she'll have a tremendous influence on the twins?"

In agreement, Francine nodded. "Heaven knows that it will be one turbulent journey, and we'll revel in every glorious moment of it!"

A New Beginning

CPSIA information can be obtained at www.ICGtesting.com
Printed in the USA
LVOW13s0755200314

378101LV00003B/4/P